"Did you hear me?"

She jumped, startled from the past, his deep voice bringing momentary panic. "I'm sorry."

He frowned at her.

She forced a smile, grimace, whatever. "I wasn't paying attention."

"We're going to have to figure out what to do. If you don't go talk to the police—"

She shot to her feet. "I already told y—"

"I know." He held up his hands, butter knife gripped in one, in a gesture of surrender. "I'm not saying you should, I'm just saying we have to figure out what we're going to do if you don't."

She lifted a brow and kept her expression serious, suppressing the genu̶i̶n̶e̶ ̶s̶m̶i̶l̶e̶ ̶t̶h̶a̶t̶ "We?"

He grinned. "W̶

Jace obviously ̶ she ignored the flutter that ̶

Phoenix jumped t̶o̶ ̶h̶i̶s̶ feet, hackles raised, a low growl rumbling in his chest.

Jace turned off the stove and slid the saucepan off the burner. Eyeing the big dog with its teeth bared, he hit the button to turn off the oven. "Get down."

Deena Alexander grew up in a small town on eastern Long Island where she lived until last year when she relocated to Clermont, Florida, with her husband, three children, son-in-law and four dogs. Now she enjoys long walks in nature all year long, despite the occasional alligator or snake she sometimes encounters. Her love for writing developed when her youngest son was born and didn't sleep through the night.

Books by Deena Alexander

Love Inspired Suspense

Crime Scene Connection

Visit the Author Profile page at Harlequin.com.

CRIME SCENE CONNECTION

DEENA ALEXANDER

LOVE INSPIRED SUSPENSE
INSPIRATIONAL ROMANCE

LOVE INSPIRED® SUSPENSE
INSPIRATIONAL ROMANCE

ISBN-13: 978-1-335-40499-2

Recycling programs
for this product may
not exist in your area.

Crime Scene Connection

Love Inspired
22 Adelaide St. West, 40th Floor
Toronto, Ontario M5H 4E3, Canada
www.Harlequin.com

Printed in U.S.A.

Judge not, and ye shall not be judged:
condemn not, and ye shall not be condemned: forgive,
and ye shall be forgiven.
—Luke 6:37

To my husband and my children, you are my world.
Thank you for always being there for me.
With all my love, forever and always.

ONE

"No. Oh no." Addison Keller scrolled past picture after picture, fear choking her. *Oh, God, please don't let this be happening again.*

"What's wrong?"

She jumped at her agent's voice and fumbled the phone. "Uh…"

No way could she tell Ron about the email. He was already freaked out enough about the death threats she'd received. "Nothing. Just upset about all of this."

"Stay where you are. I'll be there within the hour."

"No, Ron…wait. I—"

"Listen to me, Addison. This isn't a joke. I don't know exactly what's going on, but a news reporter has already made the connection to you, and the police can't be far behind. They've already questioned you once about the last murder. Do you really want to deal with them again?" The pitch of Ron's voice increased with the volume.

She scrolled back up to the first image. The email contained twelve photos. In the first two, the victim— if Addison allowed herself to think of the victim as a woman, she'd lose her battle against nausea—was still alive. The other ten had been taken after she was killed, the crime scene all too familiar, since Addison had created it in her novel.

"Ron, I don't—"

"I'm already in the car, but even in the middle of the night, with no traffic, it'll still take me an hour to get there." His heavy breathing faded in and out over the spotty cell phone connection. He muttered something unintelligible. "I'll never understand why you insist on living all the way out on Long Island."

She ran a shaky fingertip over the woman's hair on the computer screen. The same long dark hair as the rest of the victims Addison had conjured up. Guilt hammered her. If she hadn't written that book, the killer might never have chosen these victims.

"Throw some stuff together. We'll put you in a hotel somewhere if you don't want to stay with me." He ended the call without waiting for a response.

"No, no, no." Without taking her eyes from the laptop screen, she tossed the phone onto the bed, wrapped her arms around herself and doubled over, tears stinging her eyes. She blinked them back. Crying wouldn't help. She had to calm down, had to think. Had to remember what had happened when— *No.* She slammed the door on the memories trying to surface. Remembering her past wouldn't help. It would only make this nightmare real.

She squinted and pulled the laptop closer. The attention to detail in the photos laid out the crime scene exactly as she'd imagined it. She had no doubt the murder weapon, a small handgun, would be found under the overturned kitchen chair. Right where she had placed it in her book.

Unable to tear her gaze from the screen, she fumbled a hand across the nightstand, knocking over her tea in search of the remote. When her fingers closed around it, she pulled it back and turned on the TV. *Breaking News* jumped off the screen, slamming into her. She turned up the volume.

"Details are just starting to emerge on the murder that took place earlier tonight in the exclusive suburb…" Yellow crime scene tape stretched across a lawn, and cops moved in and out of the house, creating a beehive of activity.

She tuned out the rest and hit the button to turn off the TV. It didn't matter. She could, no doubt, describe the exact layout of the kitchen in the house pictured on the screen—even what wasn't visible in the photographs included with the email.

It was only a matter of time before the police knocked on her door. Again. Only this time, that arrogant detective might do more than just glare at her with suspicion darkening his eyes. This time, he'd most likely arrest her.

A creak tore her attention from the computer screen. It was a sound she knew all too well. The third step had always creaked like that.

And the killer had already made it clear he was coming for her in his previous email. No way was she waiting around to give him a target.

She flung the blanket back, toppling the computer to the side, and launched herself from the bed. No time to get changed. She stuffed her feet into the UGG boots she'd toed off when she came upstairs. Where'd her cell phone go? No idea. Forget it.

She shoved the second-story window open, praying fervently it wouldn't squeak, swung her legs over, gripped the ledge, then dropped to the ground. Ten feet. That was all the ground she had to cover before the thick woods would swallow her up. She ran. The pounding of her heart and the blood rushing through her head merged together, the thunderous noise drowning out any sounds of possible pursuit.

When she reached the woods, she slid as quietly as possible into the darkness, trying not to disturb the dense underbrush. Leaves crunched beneath her feet, and she fought desperately against the urge to flee. Bumbling through the woods in the dark on the carpet of fallen leaves would only draw the intruder's attention. Instead, she slipped into the deepest shadows with a desperate prayer the darkness would conceal her presence and the stranger would leave.

She pressed her back against a huge oak tree, then bent at the waist and braced her hands on her knees. Her chest ached, and she finally dared to take a breath. The salty scent of the sea, usually comforting, only fueled her nausea. She slapped a hand over her nose and mouth. Vomiting now would be a death sentence.

When she'd regained some semblance of control, Addison turned to face the tree. She pressed her forehead against the cool, damp bark. *This can't be happening.* Except, it was happening. And if she couldn't find a way to stop it, she was going to be the final victim of a deranged killer. Heaving in one more deep breath and holding it, Addison peeked around the tree, scraping her forehead on the rough trunk. She winced at the sting.

She couldn't say for sure the shape silhouetted in her bedroom window was a man, but the broad shoulders gave a distinctly masculine appearance. A shiver crawled up her spine. Whoever it was didn't seem to be in any hurry to follow her, ignoring the open window she'd obviously escaped through to focus on something in the room.

If it was the police in the house, she should probably

go back and talk to them. And say what, that she was responsible for the murder of the woman who had died earlier? Just like she was responsible for the woman who was killed last week. And the woman who'd be killed next week and every week thereafter until…

No. She couldn't go back. Police officers were probably not in the habit of sneaking into people's houses unannounced, in the wee hours of the morning. And there was a distinct possibility the killer was a cop—or, at the very least, someone close to the investigation. Someone who could be framing her right now while she cowered behind a tree watching him. *Oh, please, Lord, help me get out of here alive.*

She turned to flee and barreled straight into a broad chest. Her heart stopped and a vise gripped her lungs and squeezed hard.

A large hand covered her mouth before she could let loose the scream welling in her lungs. The man's hot breath bathed her neck when he whispered, "Please, don't scream. I'm here to help."

She nodded, giving up any hope of escaping his grasp.

"We have to get out of here. Now."

At least that was something they could agree on.

"I'm going to take my hand off your mouth and release you. Please, don't scream."

Heaving in a deep, shaky breath through her nose, she held his gaze and nodded again. Shadows concealed his eyes. Who was he? Cop? Accomplice? Murderer? Maybe he was just a good citizen who'd seen her climb out the window while he was prowling the neighborhood dressed all in black, had guessed she was in trouble and come to her rescue. Yeah, right. She closed her eyes and let her head fall back against the tree.

He released his hold.

The instant his hand left her, she whirled to flee.

He caught her arm and leaned close. "You're going to get us both killed."

She chanced a quick glance over her shoulder. The dim light filling her bedroom window was gone, leaving the room in complete darkness. Panic gripped her. Where'd the intruder go?

Her stranger guided her against the tree, angling his body between her and anyone who might enter the woods from the direction of the house. "Connor Bynes sent me."

Connor? She didn't know her sister's husband, but she thought he was in the military or something. Not a cop. That she knew for sure. It didn't make sense. "Why?"

"I'll explain later. Somewhere safer." He surveyed the yard and the house and glanced over his shoulder at the route through the woods her mind begged him to take. Returning his gaze to the yard, he backed away and pulled a handgun from the small of his back, then pressed a finger to his lips.

Like she'd really talk right now.

Keeping the gun aimed past the tree toward the yard, he backed a few steps deeper into the woods and gestured her toward him.

Trust him or not? Was he the answer to her desperate plea for help, or was he a threat? None of this made sense, but neither did standing there waiting for a killer to find her.

A crash broke the unnatural silence of the night, followed by the barking of the neighbor's rottweiler.

Addison dropped to a crouch and studied the yard. Moonlight spilled through the trees, the soft sea breeze rippling the leaves and sending shadows skittering across the small patch of back lawn. Hopefully, the motion would be enough to cover their movements as they fled. A deepening shadow at the back of the house caught her attention. Someone?

She only hesitated another second, her gaze focused on the man standing before her, perfectly still, as if he had all night. This wasn't the time for life-and-death decisions. Once she was somewhere safer, where she could think more clearly, she'd decide what to do. She stood and crept toward him, careful to tread lightly on the dead leaves, every crunch spearing her with a new pang of fear.

He turned and led her deeper into the woods. How on earth did he walk so quietly?

She struggled to keep him in sight and still watch where she was going. A twig beneath her foot snapped, the crack echoing through the night. She froze.

"Go." With the need for stealth blown, he gestured her ahead of him. "Run."

A blast of gunfire split the night, the thud of bullets tearing through the brush way too close.

She ran.

A grunt at her back made her pause, a barely perceptible hesitation, but her stranger propelled her forward as he returned fire.

Branches clutched her pajama sleeves, tore the thin fabric, scratched her arms and back and caught in her hair. Still, she ran, the sound of her stranger's harsh breaths keeping pace just behind her oddly comforting. The next shot brought a sharp sting as a piece of bark ricocheted into her cheek.

Jace Montana ducked to avoid getting slapped in the face by a branch Addison swung behind her as she ran. The thick stand of pine trees offered decent cover, but the branches were murder to dodge. No matter. A few cuts and scratches were nothing compared to the bullet wound in his left side. Hopefully, it was minor, even though it hurt like mad, but no way was he slowing down and holstering his weapon to check. He'd examine it later, once they were safe.

The peal of sirens tore through the night. Great. Cops. Just what he needed. This mission just went from bad to infinitely worse. He collided with an oncoming branch, which gouged his face, narrowly missing his right eye. How had he gotten himself into this mess?

Oh. Right. Connor Bynes. He'd have to remember to punch him in the mouth later. If they ever got out of this.

The sirens grew louder, coming closer. Someone must have reported the gunshots. Maybe the neighbor with the barking dog. He prayed whoever was chasing them would turn tail and run, but with the way the night was going so far, well…

Connor's warning to be discreet, not to get caught watching her—by her, the person stalking her, or by the police—rang in his head. He'd already blown the first part by having to come to her aid. He had no intention of running into anyone else. At least, not until after he'd spoken to Connor and found out more about what was going on.

"I…need a…second. Can't…breathe." Addison stopped abruptly and bent at the waist, and he plowed into her, knocking her to the ground, barely catching himself against a tree as he tripped over her sprawled form.

"Shhh…" He tried to block out the screaming of the sirens and concentrate on the sounds of the night. No use. The throbbing in his side wouldn't allow him to focus on anything else.

Tilting her head, Addison remained quiet, studying him in the moonlight.

Wait a minute. Why was the moonlight suddenly so bright? He looked around. They'd made it to the edge of the woods. He holstered his gun and pressed his fingers tentatively to his side. They came away wet with blood. Ignoring the pain, he wiped his hand on the leg of his black jeans, then crouched and crept closer to Addison. He pressed his lips to her ear. "My car's parked at the edge of a dirt road a little ways down. Do you know it?"

She nodded, her breathing ragged, then opened her mouth as if to speak.

Something heavy crunched in the dead leaves. Close. Too close.

Moving as silently as possible, he put a finger to his lips and guided her into the shadows of the brush along the side of the narrow road. Her eyes widened in fear, and he hated himself for causing it. He needed a moment to explain why he was there, to reassure her he wouldn't hurt her, to gain her trust.

But not with a killer on their heels.

He inhaled deeply, desperate for even a second or two to catch his breath. His heart thundered against his ribs.

A tear tipped over her lower lashes and tracked down her cheek. Tremors tore through her.

He had to shove the compassion aside, needed to think clearly, without heightened emotions or pain clouding his judgment. He'd do well to remember who this woman was. That should make it easy enough to keep any sympathy at bay. He pressed his lips against her ear, his voice so low she'd have to strain to hear it. "Please trust me. He's too close. If you run, we probably won't get out of this. Understand?"

Her back straightened, and she turned her sharp gaze on him, their noses a fraction of an inch apart.

"Will you stay quiet and follow me?" Urgency beat at him. The need to remain as silent as possible warred with his desire to get her to relax and trust him. If the fierce determination in her eyes was any indication, this woman didn't trust easily. And they were about out of time. Still, he froze, allowing her a moment to decide. He'd promised Connor he'd keep her safe, and one way or another, that was exactly what he intended to do.

She squeezed her eyes closed, took a deep breath, then opened them and nodded.

They'd already wasted enough time. He eased away from the bushes, pulling his gun and crouching low, careful to keep hidden in the shadows. Taking her hand in his, he started along the grass bordering the woods. They didn't have far to go, less than a quarter of a mile if his estimate was accurate. Of course, his thinking was becoming a little muddled, so he could possibly be a little—or completely—off.

Even so, creeping furtively through the shadows came second nature to him, between the amount of time he'd spent in the woods while growing up on Long Island and his time spent with the police force, and it might have worked if he'd been alone, but Addison stood up a little too high.

A bullet whizzed past them, barely missing her head. He yanked her down, throwing himself over her as he returned fire.

Blue and red lights bathed the night as a police cruiser rounded a curve down the road.

Jace rolled with Addison into the brush, grinding his teeth together to stifle a groan as sticks, rocks and dead leaves clawed his injured side. He came to rest beside her, his face planted against the ground. Sucking in a mouthful of sand and dirt, he started to choke, then froze, straining to hear even the slightest noise.

Someone crashed through the woods in the opposite direction. Apparently, the police car had scared off their attacker. But they were on borrowed time. He grabbed Addison by the arm and pulled her up. Jace was sorry there wasn't a moment to gain her trust, but saving her was more important. "Stay close to the woods on the side of the road. If you see or hear anyone, dive in. Now run."

With no hesitation, she did as he said.

He followed on her heels. They had to make it to the car and get out of there before the cops stopped them. Connor's warning had been very specific—no cops. And Connor was a private investigator with plenty of friends in high places. If he had wanted the police involved, Jace was the last person he'd have called. After being forced to resign from the Suffolk County Police Department amid a cloud of accusations about activities he'd had no involvement in, and losing the love of his life, his wife, Jennifer—the thought of which still brought a pang of grief and guilt that robbed him of breath—Jace had no use for anyone in the SCPD.

"Psst." Addison stood staring at him, her expression guarded. "Is that the dirt road you meant?"

Jace hadn't realized she'd stopped running and was gesturing across the street toward the narrow dirt road where he'd parked the borrowed Subaru Outback—what he'd thought would be a discreet, everyday car that wouldn't draw attention. Except, of course, in the dead of night, fleeing from a scene where gunshots had just been fired. That could possibly make it stand out a little.

He held his breath. Crickets chirped, a dog barked in the distance, too far away to be of any concern to him, and a foghorn sounded across the bay. He nodded toward Addison and jogged across the street, fishing the keys from his left pocket as they approached the car. Still holding the weapon, he used his left hand to slide the key into the lock.

A low growl brought him up short.

"It's all right, Phoenix. She's with me."

The big German shepherd relaxed.

"Down, boy."

He followed the command instantly, dropping to lie across the back seat, keeping his head up. Alert.

Once Jace slid into the driver's seat, he unlocked the door for Addison. He'd already disabled the interior lights. He eased his door closed as quietly as possible.

Addison did the same. When she started to buckle her seat belt, he reached out a hand to stop her. "Get down."

Her eyes widened, but she obeyed immediately, sliding lower in the seat. "Is someone out there?"

He hadn't meant to frighten her, just wanted to keep her safe—at least until he could arrange to dump her with Connor. Then he'd tend to his bullet wound and return to his life of misery, compliments of Addison and her sister, Maris. "No. Just stay low until we get out of here."

He started the car, rolled up the windows he'd left partially open for Phoenix, and shifted into Drive.

Keeping her head below window level couldn't have been easy and didn't look comfortable, but Addison didn't complain. She didn't say anything.

With the headlights off, Jace rolled slowly to the end of the dirt road, looked both ways and pulled out onto the side street. The sun would begin to rise soon, and he would lose the cover of darkness. They'd have to be long gone before that happened. He flipped on his headlights as they made a right onto the two-lane road. He glanced at Addison in the glow of the streetlights. She was holding it together.

Phoenix still lay quietly on the back seat, waiting patiently for Jace to release him.

"Okay, boy."

The big German shepherd sat up and poked his head between the seats. He nudged Jace's shoulder and whimpered, likely disturbed by the scent of blood.

"It's all right, boy."

Keeping her head low, Addison eyed the dog warily.

"This is Phoenix. He's friendly." At least he was friendly to people Jace deemed trustworthy.

She reached out a tentative hand for him to sniff, then gave him a few hesitant strokes on the head.

Jace returned his attention to the road ahead and holstered his gun. Connor should have called by now. He fished his cell phone out of his pocket and turned it on. Three missed calls. All from Connor. What a surprise.

A car sped toward them from behind. Its high beams reflected off the phone's screen, blinding him for an instant, and he swerved as it flew past.

Addison gasped, her gaze riveted on his blood-covered hand clutching the phone.

TWO

"Is that blood?" Addison motioned toward the reddish-brown streaks covering the stranger's hand as he fumbled the phone.

He spread his fingers wide, as if noticing the blood for the first time. "Yeah."

Addison waited. "Are you hurt?"

He frowned and scrolled through something on the phone. "I'm okay."

Phoenix whined.

"It's okay, boy." She turned on her side so she could reach him, careful to keep her head low, and smoothed her hand along the side of his face.

He had long hair for a German shepherd, his face more black than tan. He studied her for a moment, leaning his head into her hand, before returning his attention to his owner. He whined again.

The stranger scratched beneath Phoenix's chin. "Relax, boy. I'm fine."

She couldn't tell if the statement was true or if he was just trying to soothe the dog's obvious unease.

"Lie down, now."

Phoenix snorted and rested his chin on his paws. If it was possible for a dog to sulk, he did.

Streetlights illuminated the interior each time they passed beneath one, casting light over the man's hard features and then plunging them back into shadows. There was something familiar about him, though she was quite certain they'd never met before. "Who are you?"

"A friend of Connor's." His jaw clenched.

She waited, but he didn't elaborate. A dizzying array of questions swirled through her mind. "Why would Connor send you to help me? How would he have even known I was in trouble?"

The man ignored her questions and pressed the phone to his ear. His harsh breathing echoed through the small space.

"Can you at least tell me your name?"

"Jace." He pressed the end button and slammed the phone into the cupholder in the center console with a little more force than necessary, then shoved his hand through the dark, shaggy hair that brushed the collar of his shirt. He glanced in the rearview mirror as he entered the nearly deserted expressway.

Reality knifed through her, cramping her gut. There was no doubt she was being stalked by a ruthless killer, and here she was, locked in a car with a complete stranger and a giant dog on a deserted road in the wee hours of the morning. She shot up in the seat. "Let me out."

Phoenix's head popped up, his ears standing erect.

Jace spared her a quick glance, checked the rearview mirror, then returned his attention to the road, keeping the speedometer pegged at exactly sixty. Just enough over the speed limit not to draw attention but not enough to get pulled over. "Please, just give me a minute, and we'll talk."

Maybe she should just fling the door open and throw herself out. A narrow stretch of woods bordered the side of the road, separating the six-lane highway from the surrounding neighborhoods. Surely she could find help fairly quickly?

Phoenix settled back down.

Addison sighed and dropped back against the seat. Even if she could outrun Jace, her chances of outrunning the dog were nil.

She closed her eyes and reminded herself there was a time to be quiet and a time to speak. Maybe he was so quiet because he was praying. Or injured too badly to talk. Or concentrating. Or worried about something. And she was making it more difficult for him by demanding answers. Jace had appeared just as she'd prayed for deliverance. If she couldn't trust him, she should at least have faith in God.

With Jace's attention split evenly between watching the road ahead and checking the rearview mirror, he hit the lock button. "Get down."

She slid to the floor. Headlights reflected from the side-view mirror as a car barreled up behind them. Red and blue lights washed over the interior.

The police. Her instincts kicked in, demanding she signal for help. But even as she started to rise, his hand settled on her shoulder. It didn't matter. She wouldn't have signaled anyway. At least Jace *might* turn out to be…safe.

When she'd received the first email from the killer a week ago, she'd thought it was some sort of a sick joke, then maybe an elaborate scheme to unnerve her. When she'd flipped on the twenty-four-hour news channel and spent the night watching the eerily familiar scene unfold, she'd been forced to accept the reality that a killer had targeted her.

Though she'd considered going to the police then, fear of her ex-husband, Brandon Carlisle, and his associates had held her immobile. Brandon, a high-ranking, horribly corrupt chief in the Suffolk County Police Department, wielded a tremendous amount of power, and their marriage had ended badly. His cronies had harassed her relentlessly after the divorce, despite the fact Brandon had been the one to file.

Once the authorities had connected her book to the first killing and arrived on her doorstep, she'd cooperated fully, answering all of their questions, ignoring their disbelieving expressions, being as honest as she could.

Until Detective Marshall Brooks had interrogated her. That interview had been the game changer. She remembered Marshall from several events she'd attended during her marriage. He was a good friend of Brandon's and, no doubt, a member of his posse. The arrogant detective had swaggered into her kitchen with a chip on his shoulder and a gleam of anticipation in his eyes before he'd cut her apart, openly accusing her of lying and conspiring with a killer to promote her book.

Letting the cops get ahold of her would be a terrible mistake.

She was about to tell Jace not to pull over when the cruiser flew past them.

"Sorry." The pressure of his hand eased. "It's safe to get up now."

She swiped the tears tracking down her face and sat in the seat, buckling the seat belt without acknowledging him. Silence weighed heavily, a physical barrier between them. Lowering her head, she massaged her temples, desperate to ease the constant throbbing so she could think.

"Look, I'm sorry. I didn't mean to scare you. Connor barely gave me any information when he called, but the one thing he was adamant about, other than making sure you were safe, was not involving the police." Jace glanced at her, sighed and shifted position, concern etched in the deep lines bracketing his mouth. "And now I can't reach him."

She nodded. Connor would know her history with Brandon, since her sister, Maris, had tried, and failed, to take him down. Her head pounded in time with the steady rhythm of the tires against the pavement.

The phone rang, and she jumped, the sound deafening in the confines of the silent car. She pressed a hand against her chest and leaned back against the seat.

Jace grabbed the phone on the first ring. "I have her, and before you ask, I know I was only supposed to keep an eye on her, but when I found her fleeing her bedroom window with a killer on her heels, I figured you'd want me to intervene."

The mumbling of what sounded like a man's voice echoed through the car, but she couldn't make out any actual words.

"What are you talking about? That wasn't part of the deal, man." His breath wheezed out between clenched teeth, and he winced and leaned toward his door. "No."

Remembering he was injured, possibly badly, intruded on her fear, but didn't lessen her curiosity.

"Lis—"

The volume of the mutters from the other end of the line increased, the caller's sense of urgency apparent.

"No, Con—"

Silence returned. Jace pulled the phone from his ear

and stared at it for a moment, then lowered it gently to the cupholder and dropped it in. He returned his hand to the wheel, his grip tightening the tendons in his hands. "Okay, can you please tell me what's going on?"

Surprise held her tongue.

"I can't help you if I have no information," he insisted. "The whole story, not just an urgent plea from Connor in the middle of the night to protect you until he can get there."

She shook her head, still trying to wrap her head around Connor's involvement. How had he even known she was in trouble? She couldn't remember, but she thought Ron might have said something over the phone before she'd jumped out her window, about a reporter connecting the murders to her novel. It seemed like they'd spoken ages ago, but in reality, it was probably not more than an hour or so. If what Ron had said was true, how much did Connor know?

Since her sister, Connor's wife, was an investigative journalist with quite a list of accomplishments to her credit, it was possible Maris had heard something, even though she and Addison hadn't spoken in several years. The sisters had fallen out after Maris had written a scathing article about Addison's ex-husband without even giving her a heads-up. But had they read Addison's book? Did they realize the danger Maris was in? She'd have to get in touch with them, warn them, if they didn't already know. She turned her gaze on Jace.

"Look…" He tilted his head from side to side and rolled his shoulders. "I want to help, but my hands are tied if no one will tell me what's happening. Please."

Help? The small flare of hope dimmed almost immediately. No one could help her. She'd do well to accept that. Now that the immediate danger had passed, though, her curiosity about Connor's involvement was piqued. "What did Connor tell you?"

"Nothing." His jaw clenched in what she was beginning to recognize was a sign of agitation. Or possibly pain.

The fact he'd been hurt trying to help her gnawed at her. "Are you all right?"

"I'll be fine." He blew out a breath and leaned a bit to the side, and his posture relaxed. "Connor called a few hours ago. He didn't give any details of what was going on, but he said he needed a favor. He told me he had reason to believe you were in danger and asked if I would watch the house discreetly until he could get there."

He shrugged, as if it were the most natural thing in the world.

Maybe for him it was perfectly normal to go out in the middle of the night with a loaded gun, leave his car hidden, and crouch in the woods outside a woman's window. Her hand shook as she swiped her tangled hair behind her ear. It didn't seem he was being purposely evasive, more like he just didn't have any information to give her. "I don't understand."

"Don't understand what?"

Anything. Probably better to keep that to herself. "Didn't you question Connor?"

"Yeah. I asked him who you were."

"And when he told you, you said yes? Just like that? Why would you do that when you don't even know me?"

The deep timbre of his laughter startled her. "Actually, when he told me who you were, I said no."

She stared at him, unsure what to say.

"I owe Connor big-time, and there's nothing I wouldn't do for him, despite the issues between us. So here I am, helping Maris Halloway's sister." He lowered his gaze and shook his head before returning his attention to the road ahead. "Who'd have thought?"

She barely caught the last comment as he mumbled it under his breath. Obviously, there was some problem between him and her sister. Maybe he was an exboyfriend or something. He seemed like her type. Maris always had gone for the bad boys. And there was no mistaking the danger practically radiating from him. "So…now what?"

He squinted as he checked something in front of the steering wheel. "First, we have to stop for gas. Then… I don't know yet. Connor was supposed to meet me, but he got held up."

"Where is he?"

"Out of town on a case."

"But he's on his way back?"

"Yeah. But something happened." He frowned and glanced at the phone, which remained silent. "And before you ask, he didn't say what."

She huffed out a breath and slouched in the seat, exhaustion finally weighing on her now that the adrenaline surge had subsided. She needed rest and time to think. She needed peace to pray and listen. She needed to check her email. "I have a cabin."

The cabin she'd had Ron buy reminded her he was on his way. She had to get in touch with him.

Jace shook his head. "We have to go someplace no one will find you until we figure out what's going on."

"No one knows about the cabin." She'd considered trying to buy it through a dummy corporation, but Brandon would probably have been able to find it that way. The last thing she needed was to spend her time there looking over her shoulder. Though she didn't fully trust

Ron, since he most often seemed to have his own best interests at heart, he'd done right by her as far as her writing career. So she'd "loaned" him the money and asked him to buy the cabin for her. The arrangement had worked out well enough. She got peace when she needed an escape, and he got a cabin he could use when he wanted. A win-win for both of them.

Jace remained quiet, staring straight ahead. Whether he was ignoring her or contemplating her offer, she had no idea.

"I bought it last year so I would have someplace to go if I wanted…privacy. I didn't want anyone to be able to find me, so it's under another name." Not only did the log cabin in the mountains offer the solitude she sometimes needed and the perfect place to hide if she wanted to avoid being found, she also had a computer there.

"How far?"

A glimmer of hope flickered. "About six hours."

Checking his mirrors again, he continued driving in silence, except for her occasionally offering directions.

Despite the air of danger surrounding him, his strong profile brought a sense of comfort she didn't understand. His presence made her feel safe, like she wasn't alone. He made her lower her guard—a mistake that could prove deadly for both of them.

He'd already been injured trying to help her. Two women had already been killed because of a story she'd written. She wouldn't have Jace's death on her conscience, as well.

She hardened her resolve. She had to get away from him. As soon as she did, she'd contact Maris, then find a way to call Ron. He could drop a car off somewhere close by for her, then she could head up to the cabin alone. That was the only way she could keep everyone else safe. Well, she might not be able to keep everyone safe, but she'd save as many people as she could. With an eye toward escape, she gestured to the upcoming exit sign. "There's a gas station up the road here."

He hit the turn signal and left the highway.

"It's on the right." She couldn't control the tremor in her voice. Hopefully, he wouldn't notice.

As he approached the gas station, he pointed toward the back. "Could you please grab my jacket from the back seat?"

Unbuckling her seat belt, she turned and grabbed a dark windbreaker from the seat behind him.

Phoenix rolled onto his side. As long as he left the dog in the car, her plan—if you could call it that—should work.

"Thanks." He took the jacket from her. "Could you hold the wheel a minute? I don't want to waste any time."

While she held the wheel steady, he struggled to shrug into the jacket. A low hiss reminded her he was injured. She buried the guilt. He could go for help as soon as he was rid of her.

"Slow down." She studied the woods behind the gas station. She'd have to be fast. At this time of morning, the station would be empty. It would only take a minute or two for him to go in, pay for the gas and return to the car. Unless he used a credit card. If he paid at the pump, her plan was shot. Her hand grew slick on the wheel. Using a credit card would be foolish, leaving a trail and all that. He definitely didn't strike her as foolish.

The cool touch of metal against her wrist ripped her attention from the patch of woods. Before she could pull her hand away, the handcuff clicked closed.

"What do you think you're doing?"

Hooking the other end to the steering wheel, he grinned. "Just making sure I don't lose you. Connor was pretty adamant about keeping you safe."

He rolled into the lot, scanning the area as he approached the pump. When he stopped, his expression turned serious. "Don't cause a scene here. Please."

Sitting under the bright lights, she was able to see his eyes clearly for the first time. For some reason she'd expected them to be brown, but he had the bluest eyes she'd ever seen. Deep, dark blue, like the depths of the ocean, and just as dangerous.

"Phoenix, stay." He grabbed his phone, stuffed it into his jacket pocket and climbed from the car.

"Hey. Where are you going?" Was he seriously leaving her handcuffed to the steering wheel?

His laughter was cut off as he slammed the door.

Traffic began to increase as they headed off Long Island. If he didn't hurry, they'd soon be immersed in the snarl of rush hour on the Long Island Expressway. He stepped a little harder on the accelerator.

Addison sat still, staring through the windshield, arms crossed, silence blaring. She hadn't said a word since he'd gotten back in the car at the gas station. It wasn't like he hadn't uncuffed her once they'd gotten back on the highway. Steering with her cuffed to the wheel—and completely uncooperative—had been quite an ordeal. He bit back a smile. He had a feeling she might not appreciate the humor in the situation just yet.

She shot him a scowl as if she could read the amusement in his thoughts.

"My jacket is on the back seat if you're cold." He'd put the heat on when he'd returned to the car and found her shivering, but she'd ignored the offer of his jacket then, so he'd tossed it onto the back seat. He started to reach into the back, but a flare of pain from his side stopped him. A quick stop in the gas station men's room had assured him the bullet wound wasn't much more than a graze, but he still needed to clean and bandage it as soon as possible. And it still hurt like mad.

He hit the turn signal and left the Long Island Expressway behind in favor of the Cross Island Parkway, then checked his phone again, even though he knew full well he hadn't missed any calls.

He'd known Connor most of his life, but hadn't seen him since he'd announced he was going to marry Maris Halloway. He still couldn't think of her as Maris Bynes. Knowing how Jace felt about Maris, there was no way Connor would have asked him to babysit her sister if the stakes weren't life or death. Though he'd applauded Maris's efforts to expose Addison's ex-husband and Jace's ex-partner and one-time friend, Brandon Carlisle, for the snake he was, she'd gone too far, implicating Jace in crimes he'd had no part in and no knowledge of. The woman had destroyed his life by going public with allegations that simply weren't true.

He rolled his shoulders, hoping to relieve some of the tension knotting his muscles, and tried to shake off his concern about the ominous silence from his cell phone. He turned his attention to Addison's silence. It was past time for her to start talking.

"Do you want something to eat or drink?" He gestured toward the brown paper bag balanced across the cupholders between them.

If looks could kill, he'd have dropped right there, probably sending the Outback sailing off the Throgs Neck Bridge.

"Look, I'm not going to apologize." He didn't feel

bad about cuffing her, since he'd promised Connor he'd keep her safe and her intention to run had been clearly written all over her delicate features. Though he did have to admit a certain amount of regret that she was so angry about it. It wasn't like he'd left her defenseless with Phoenix in the back seat. "I have no idea what's going on here, except that Connor asked me to sit on you until he can get here. I can only assume he'll explain more when he arrives."

She nodded and returned her attention to staring at the highway.

He dug a water bottle from the brown paper bag, opened it and took a mouthful. So what if she didn't want to talk. Better for him if she just sat quietly until he could meet up with Connor. "It might help me keep you safe if I knew what was going on."

She blew out a breath and her rigid posture relaxed. "I don't know what's happening, except that a killer seems to have based his murders on the murders from a book I wrote. And I certainly don't understand what Connor's involvement would be—I don't even know him. And I didn't think Maris even knew I wrote a book."

She shook her head, then dug through the bag and pulled out a bottle of water and a package of ibuprofen. She shot him a grateful look.

He grinned. "Does that mean I'm forgiven for the handcuff incident?"

"Don't try my patience, mister." A small smile played at the corner of her mouth before it settled into a frown. Lowering her head, she massaged her temples. "Can I please use your phone?"

"What do you need the phone for?" Not that he wouldn't let her use it, but he had to be careful.

She tilted her head and lifted a brow. "Because I need to make a call."

"You know you can't tell anyone where you are, right?"

"My agent was on his way to my house. He's probably there already and in a total panic that he can't find me."

"Okay. But please keep it short. Don't tell him where you are. Don't tell him where you're going. Just tell him you're safe and leave it at that. Okay?" As much as he wanted to trust her judgment, her safety was critical, and he didn't know who her agent was. Actually, he didn't have any background information on her or her associates at all.

"Yes, sir." She rolled her eyes as she held her hand out for the phone.

"And hit star sixty-seven before you dial. You're safer for the moment if no one can figure out who you're with." Jace grinned and pulled the phone from his pocket, but when she grabbed it, he gripped it tighter. "And after you finish, you'll answer my questions?"

Holding his gaze with hers, she nodded once and took the phone. Her leg bounced repeatedly while she dialed and pressed the phone to her ear. "Come on, come on…"

"Would you mind putting it on speaker?"

She lifted a brow.

"Sorry, I'd like to be able to judge his reactions. Until we understand more about what's going on, it's safer for everyone to limit the number of people involved."

She nodded. "I can understand that."

Odd she didn't jump to defend her agent if they were friends. He'd have to remember to ask about their relationship.

She hit the speaker button just as Ron answered. "Ron, it's Addison. Where are you?"

"Where are *you*? I've been trying to call for the past half hour. There are cops all over your house."

"Did you talk to them?"

"No. I tried to call you first."

So the man had arrived at a woman's house in the middle of the night and found cops all over the place, but he didn't go in to see what was going on? Didn't check to see if she was hurt, or worse, even when he couldn't reach her by phone?

"All right." Addison took a deep breath and massaged the bridge of her nose.

"What's going on? Where are you?" Though Ron's voice remained level, his tension vibrated through the connection.

"I'm fine." She glanced at Jace. "I'm with a friend of a friend. I can't say where I'm going right now, but I'm safe."

He paused for a moment. "How will I get in touch with you?"

"I'll call when I can."

"I need to be able to reach you, Addison." Annoyance crept into the man's tone. "I've already heard from your publicist and your editor. There are rumors they might delay the release of book two because of this mess."

"Uh…okay. I'll be in touch. Thanks, Ron." She ended the call over Ron's protests and handed Jace the phone without looking at him.

He took it and studied her profile, strong, determined and yet delicate and fragile. On the verge of breaking? He resisted the urge to reach out to her, to reassure her everything would be okay. He wouldn't lie to her, and, without knowing what they were up against, he had no idea what the outcome would be. "Want to tell me what's going on now?"

"What do you mean?"

"For starters, who was the man in your house?"

"I don't know."

"Take a guess. It would be much easier to protect you if I had some idea what to expect."

She tucked the tangled mess of long, auburn hair behind her ear, then swallowed two ibuprofen and half the bottle of water. "About a week ago, a woman was murdered."

Her hands shook as she recapped the bottle and pressed what was left of the cold water against her forehead. Pain contorted her features. When she next spoke, it was so quietly he had to strain to hear her over the hum of the tires against the highway. "And it was my fault."

Though it probably made him a total jerk, he couldn't help thinking that if she was anything like her sister, she could be right. Of course, he doubted Maris would show half the regret and guilt obviously plaguing her sister. "How was it your fault?"

She sighed and sat back, dropping the bottle into the cupholder. "Like I said earlier, I wrote a book. The first murder, which happened last week, mimicked the crime scene in the story exactly, down to the last detail."

"The first murder?"

"Yeah. The second copycat murder took place last night, exactly one week after the first, just like in my book. Again, the crime scene was an exact replica."

"How do you know the crime scenes match?"

She hesitated.

"I can't help you if you're not honest with me."

"It's not that I don't want to be honest, just that it's…" Tears streamed down her cheeks. "It's difficult to talk about, to even think about."

He gripped the wheel tighter to keep from reaching out and brushing her tears away, allowing her the moment she seemed to need.

She sucked in a deep, shaky breath and squeezed her eyes closed. "I received emails. They had pictures of the…scenes."

A pang of sympathy caught him off guard. "The bodies?"

She nodded, sobs racking her delicate frame. "Before…" She swallowed hard. "During and…after."

Her soft cries touched a part of him he'd thought long hardened, and he allowed her a little space. He didn't reach out to her, though he wanted to, needed to place a hand over hers to offer support and comfort and lend her the strength she would require to make it through whatever came next.

But she seemed so skittish, so wary, he was afraid she might take his gesture the wrong way. He wouldn't be able to do anything for her if she was afraid of him. He was going to have to earn her trust, and he had a feeling it wouldn't come easy.

Unfortunately, they couldn't afford to waste too much time. As soon as the sobs started to ease, he gently resumed his questioning. "Was the email address they came from familiar?"

She shook her head without looking at him. "No. They each came from different email addresses. There was nothing familiar about either of them."

"Was there a message?"

"Yes. The murder scenes from my book were written out in the body of the emails. Word for word. Even the punctuation error that somehow made its way through the entire editing process was there. The pictures were attached. And the subject line of each email was *The Final Victim.*"

"The *final* victim?"

With the heels of her hands, she rubbed her eyes. "The title of my book."

Recognition surfaced. Though he'd spent most of the past four years in a haze of self-pity, even he'd heard the name, though he couldn't remember where. "Isn't that kinda big?"

"It's been on pretty much every bestseller list since it came out six months ago."

So much for narrowing down the killer to people who'd read the book. Anyone could have read it. "What else can you tell me about the book that might help give us an idea what he'll do next?"

Addison leaned her head back against the seat and closed her eyes. If not for the occasional hitch in her breathing, he'd have thought she dozed off. She shifted to face the window, and he could no longer tell if her eyes were open or closed. "I think the most important thing is the game itself."

"Game?" If not for such dire circumstances, the thought might have intrigued him. "What do you mean?"

"The title of the book, *The Final Victim*, refers to either the lead detective or the killer."

"I don't understand. How could it refer to either of them?"

"The killer was fixated more on the detective herself than the other victims, determined to prove he could outsmart her, desperately wanting to kill her but unable to get close enough, so he devised a game to lure her out. He'd kill one woman each week until she either killed him or slipped up so he could get his shot at her. The game only ends when one of them is dead."

Definitely intriguing. His curiosity got the better of him. "Why did he want to kill her?"

"I don't know yet. I haven't gotten that far. Something from their past, though, some incident where they ran across each other before the murders started. At least, that's what I hinted at in book one. I've also alluded to the killer being a cop or crime scene investigator, someone close to the investigation, but *The Final Victim* is the first in a series, and I didn't name the killer in book one."

"So he wasn't caught?"

She shook her head.

Jace blew out a breath and leaned his head back against the headrest. "How many women does he kill in book one?"

"Five." She sobbed. "The last of which is the detective's sister."

THREE

The car door clicked shut softly, jolting Addison from her nightmare. Her eyes shot open, and she sat up straighter in the seat. She pressed her thumb and forefinger to her eyes. Not a nightmare. Reality. How she'd ever fallen asleep with the mess her life had become was beyond her.

They'd made it to the rest area just outside the small town in the valley below her cabin. Not that it was much of a rest area—a small brick building housing restrooms and a couple of vending machines and a stretch of grass with a few picnic tables. No matter, as long as it was deserted.

She squinted against the morning sun's bright rays. At least they'd made it through the night without getting caught or killed. That was a plus.

She rubbed the sleep from her eyes and flipped down the visor, relieved to find a small mirror. She opened it and cringed. A stranger's bloodshot eyes stared back at her from amid deep, puffy dark circles. She pressed a tentative finger to the small gouge in her left cheek. It stung, but not as badly as she'd expected. The scratches crisscrossing the rest of her face barely hurt. No sense even trying to tame the rat's nest of her hair without a full bottle of conditioner. She picked a few small twigs and a piece of leaf out of the mess before pushing the mirror closed and flipping up the visor.

With a quick glance around to be sure no one else had pulled in—not out of any great sense of vanity, but because the condition she was in would certainly draw attention—she opened the door and got out. Every muscle protested as she arched her back in a futile attempt to ease the stiffness. The thought of a very long, very hot shower brought her to the verge of tears.

Jace and Phoenix had walked to the far end of the small rest stop. Jace bent and picked up a stick, then tossed it across the patch of grass that made up the picnic area.

Phoenix charged after it.

The events of the night before—which had thankfully stopped battering her for a couple minutes while she'd composed herself and surveyed the damage inflicted on her—came back in a flurry of confusion, bombarding her with questions. Most important, who was Jace? Why was he here? And what involvement did he have with Connor and Ma—

Oh, no. Maris! Lord, watch over her, please. Panic held her frozen. They had to get to her sister before the killer did. And they had to find a way to identify who his next targets might be and warn them, protect them. Then they had to find the killer and stop him. Somehow. She shut the door and hurried toward Jace.

He turned in her direction, hesitated for a moment, then whistled for Phoenix.

She tried to relax. If the killer followed the story line, they had plenty of time—plenty of victims—before Maris would be in danger. But was the killer already watching her? Already searching for the perfect backdrop to imitate the scene Addison had created? And what of the women who'd come before Maris? How could she save them?

Jace started toward her with Phoenix at his side, not jogging, but moving at a brisk enough pace. Something tugged at her. There was something familiar about him, about the way he moved, the way he carried himself. She'd seen him before, at least from a distance.

Recognition slammed through her with the force of a sledgehammer, knocking the breath from her lungs. Jason Montana. She staggered backward. Why would he help her…or Maris? He wouldn't.

She turned and fled.

Phoenix barked once.

No way could she outrun the big dog. She bolted for the car. Had he left the keys in the ignition? If not, she'd keep running toward the road. Maybe someone would stop and help. On this deserted stretch of highway? Yeah, right. Unable to slow her forward momentum, she slammed into the closed passenger door, then fumbled for the handle.

Jace's harsh breaths on the back of her neck warned her she'd been too slow. "Wait."

She whirled to face him.

He bent forward a little, favoring his side, and sucked in a couple of deep breaths. "Just wait. Please."

"I know who you are."

Shaking his head, he stood straighter, catching her gaze and holding it. "It doesn't matter."

"Of course it matters." She despised the tremor in her voice but couldn't control it. "You're a cop."

"No." He clenched his teeth, working his jaw from side to side for a moment. "I *was* a cop."

"Whatever." It made no difference. Either way, he'd

been investigated with her ex, thanks to Maris. Of course, Brandon and his buddies had all been found innocent of any wrongdoing, even though they'd all been guilty of numerous crimes. The whole pack of them was crooked and corrupt, abusing their power for financial gain and sometimes just because they could. And Addison's life had become a living nightmare. A nightmare she had no intention of reliving.

"I'm outta here." She tried to move away, but he grabbed her wrist. She glanced pointedly at his hand, then returned her gaze to his, careful to maintain eye contact. No way she'd turn away first.

"Please…" He held her gaze, his eyes steady on her. "Listen to me."

Sweat slid down her back, despite the chill in the morning air. If he wouldn't release her, she had no choice but to listen, but she refused to give him the respect of acknowledging his demands.

"Look at you. You can't go traipsing down the road in half-shredded pajamas with scratches and cuts covering your face and arms and…" He frowned and reached up with his free hand to pull something out of her hair. He held a mangled leaf in front of her face. "Really? How far do you think you'll get before you're picked up by a stranger or, even worse, a cop?"

She couldn't argue with his logic, but she didn't have to like it. "Fine. I'll go as far as the cabin with you, if you can explain why you'd do anything to help me or Maris."

The crunch of tires on gravel saved him from having to answer. She and Jace both looked toward the sound, him without releasing the loose hold he still had on one of her wrists.

An old, rusted pickup truck slowed as it passed by

them on its way into the rest area. A big black dog in the bed barked.

Phoenix, who'd been patiently waiting beside Jace, growled.

"Get in the car." Jace gently guided her out of the way and opened the passenger door.

Addison stared at him.

Jace couldn't have much use for her, probably couldn't care less if she lived or died, but he had to detest Maris. Why would Connor have called him? Nothing made sense. A dull throb began at the base of her neck.

A tall man in a cowboy hat emerged from the front of the pickup, not bothering to hide his interest as he stared openly at Jace and Addison. He whistled, and his dog jumped to the ground at his side.

"Please, Addison. Get in the car and we'll talk. I'll explain everything I know, and we'll try to figure out what's happening."

The last thing Addison needed was someone recognizing her, even if it was highly doubtful anyone would, especially given her current condition. The memory of how she looked prodded her to slip into the car. She was definitely drawing too much attention. And Jace wasn't in much better shape. Cuts, scratches and welts marred his face and hands. His hair looked as if he'd shoved his fingers through it a hundred times, which he probably had, and there were still flecks of dried blood on his arm, even though he'd washed most of it off in the men's room at the gas station.

After slamming the car door shut, Jace rounded the car, lifted the seat to let Phoenix scramble into the back, then got in. Holding the newcomer's gaze, he started the car.

Addison held her breath, terrified the stranger would try to stop them, perhaps more terrified he wouldn't.

Jace waved on his way by, and the stranger returned the gesture, then stared after them as he led his dog across the small lot to the picnic area, pulled out his cell phone and made a call.

Addison pulled her gaze from the side-view mirror and studied Jace. He had come to her rescue in the middle of the night, so the least she could do was hear him out. And as yet, he hadn't given her any reason not to trust him. "Okay. Explain, then. Tell me why I should trust you."

"Connor Bynes was my best friend, like a brother to me since we were kids." Jace reentered the highway and continued to head west. He sighed and shifted in his seat. "I lost my parents when I was sixteen, and his family took me in. I lived with them until I joined the police force. We stayed close until…well…the situation with Brandon…"

He shrugged as if it was no big deal, but Addison was used to reading people. The pain etched in the lines of his face told a different story.

He didn't have to finish.

Addison had suspected Jace was guilty of some sort of corruption, even if he had gotten away with it, just because he'd once been Brandon's partner, and that wasn't fair. She didn't know him, and she was judging him based on the sins of another. She squirmed in her seat. Of course, that didn't mean he was innocent, either.

Maybe Connor had thought he was guilty, as well. "Have you spoken to him?"

"Not in the past four or five years."

The same amount of time that had passed since the

investigation, and the same amount of time Connor had been with Maris. No surprise they hadn't spoken since.

"Then, a few hours ago, he called out of nowhere. He was...stressed. More stressed than I've ever heard him. He begged me to keep an eye on your house and protect you until he could get to us. Said he had to take care of something on another case first, but he'd reach me as soon as possible."

"Take the next exit and make a left." She gestured toward the upcoming exit ramp. He was finally talking, but now she had more questions than answers. One of which outweighed everything else. Though she and Maris hadn't spoken in the same number of years, the thought of the fate awaiting Maris roiled in Addison's gut. "Did he say if Maris is okay?"

"No. I'm sorry. He didn't mention her." He glanced in the rearview mirror, and his fists tightened on the wheel, whitening his knuckles. He sat up straighter and glanced at her seat belt. "Hold on."

"What's wrong?"

He accelerated and flew past the exit ramp, then signaled and pulled into the left lane.

"Where are you going? You passed the exit."

"Don't turn around. Look in your side mirror and tell me if you recognize the car coming up in the right lane."

Addison glanced in the mirror. A silver sedan barreled toward them.

Jace increased his speed, keeping ahead of the oncoming car.

Where had he come from? Moments ago they'd been alone on the highway. "It doesn't look familiar. Is he following us?"

Jace frowned, keeping his gaze split between the highway ahead of them and the rearview mirror. "I'm pretty sure the same car was behind us before I pulled into the rest area."

"How is that possible? No one else pulled into the rest area with us except for the guy in the pickup truck." Addison clutched the sides of the seat as the speedometer crept past eighty.

"Which means, if it is the same car, he waited outside the rest stop when we pulled in. Maybe hoping to go unnoticed."

"Then why speed up and draw attention to himself now?"

Jace shrugged. "Who knows? This stretch of road is fairly deserted, and I had already signaled to exit the highway when he sped up. Maybe he was hoping to get to us before we entered a more populated area."

Get to them? Meaning what? Kill them? Addison stared in the side mirror at the car keeping pace in the right lane and slightly behind them. "Maybe he's just staying behind you, figuring if there's a police officer up ahead, he'll pull you over first."

"Only one way to find out," Jace mumbled and lifted his foot off the gas.

"What are you doing? Why are we slowing down?"

"Quick, turn around and clip the seat belt through Phoenix's harness."

She flung her seat belt off, turned and scrambled to her knees. With her gaze glued to the oncoming car, she secured the belt through the harness and clicked it shut.

The silver car accelerated and shot across into their lane.

She dropped back into her seat and secured her belt. "Go."

"Hold on." Jace hit the gas.

The car bumped them from behind.

Their back end swerved. Jace recovered easily and hit the gas. They shot ahead of their pursuer.

Addison squeezed her eyes shut and prayed.

"One mile to the next exit."

She chanced a quick look over her shoulder. "He's right on your tail."

"Brace yourself."

She braced her feet against the floor and held on.

The instant he passed the exit ramp, Jace jerked the car to the right and slammed on the brakes. As he hit the right lane, he swung the wheel around.

The world spun, and her stomach pitched.

Their back end spun a hundred eighty degrees until they were facing the wrong way on the highway.

The silver car rocketed past them and then skidded to a stop, unable to make the turn as quickly as Jace had.

Jace floored the gas and headed back toward the exit ramp. He flung the car around into another U-turn, hitting the exit ramp way too fast.

Addison gripped the armrest, certain the car had tipped onto two wheels.

He whipped the steering wheel the other way, hurtled them onto a narrow, thankfully deserted, road, spun around and hung a quick left.

Her stomach heaved as she watched the road behind them in her side mirror.

Jace made a series of seemingly random turns before finally slowing down. "I'm pretty sure I lost him."

"Now what?" Was it still safe to go to the cabin? Did the killer know where they were headed? How could he? "Do you think he followed us from the house?"

"I don't know." He pulled into a hotel parking lot and parked between a mobile home and a tractor trailer. "Are you okay?"

Was she? A little queasy but otherwise unhurt. "I think so."

He reached between the seats and petted Phoenix. "Are you okay, boy? Sorry about that."

"Do you want to unclip him and take him out?" She would definitely not complain if she could get out of the car for a minute or two. Maybe the fresh air would ease the nausea.

He looked around. "Not yet. Let's get to the cabin, then we can decide where to go from there. It shouldn't be too far."

"Do you think it's still safe to go there?"

"I have no idea, but I don't have any better ideas. Let's hope he followed us from the house and doesn't know where we're headed." With one last pat for Phoenix, he turned back around, studied their surroundings, then shifted into gear and eased from their hiding spot. "In any case, we won't be staying there long. Just long enough to get cleaned up and rest a little while, hopefully meet up with Connor."

"There are supplies at the cabin, but we'll probably need a few more things before we leave." She'd have to go into town at some point, but she couldn't go anywhere looking like this. Even though only a few of the residents knew her, in a town the size of Shady Creek, gossip was a popular pastime. In her current disheveled state, she'd be the topic of conversation for some time.

He pressed a hand against his left side. "We can worry about that later."

"You should probably try Connor again before we get any farther. We'll lose any kind of decent cell service soon." And then they'd be stranded on the side of a mountain with no way to get help.

* * *

Jace and Phoenix stood on the log cabin's wrap-around porch. The subsiding adrenaline rush, while making him jittery, was doing little to stave off the exhaustion beating at him. He ignored it. At least he'd slept a couple of hours before Connor's frantic call to protect Addison.

And thankfully, he'd gotten ahold of Connor before they headed up the mountain road to let him know exactly where to find them, and he'd confirmed Connor would be there to relieve him by nightfall. He blinked a few times to soothe the scratchiness in his eyes and admired the view. Addison hadn't been exaggerating when she said it was secluded. One of only a handful of homes dotting the narrow road as it wound its way up the mountain. "You're sure no one knows about this place?"

Addison fished a key out from beneath a flowerpot beside the door.

Jace lifted a brow but refrained from any comment about her lack of security. He was already on her bad side just from his association with her ex, and…well… it was possible the handcuff incident hadn't earned him any favor, either, though she seemed to have forgiven him for that.

Hadn't he judged her the same way? He'd assumed she'd had some involvement with her ex's crimes. She had been married to Brandon, after all, so how could she not know what he was? But he'd been the man's partner for years, and he hadn't known. Brandon Carlisle was a master at hiding the monster he was from the world.

From what Jace had seen of Addison so far, despite the fear for her own life that had to be consuming her,

her deepest concerns seemed to be for others—her sister, the other women who had been or would become targets of a killer she felt guilty for creating, though it clearly wasn't her fault. It seemed he'd possibly misjudged her as badly as she'd misjudged him.

He'd also assumed Maris had found out what Brandon was doing from Addison, and used the information to write the scathing article that had sent Internal Affairs chasing after Brandon, and she wouldn't have been wrong, if that was the case. If she had information that could take him down, she most certainly should have come forward. Brandon Carlisle needed to be punished. Problem was, he hadn't been. He'd gotten away with everything, as usual.

Instead, Jace's entire world had crumbled, because Maris had named him in her article, as well. Brandon Carlisle's partner, guilty by association. But when the time came, and he found out the accusations she'd hurled against Brandon were true, he hadn't stood with Brandon.

That wasn't Addison's fault. Or Maris's. And if he had to do it again, he still would not have stood by a man who abused his power for his own gain, extorted money and favors from those who'd initially trusted him, bribed anyone who wouldn't go along with what he wanted, blackmailed those he couldn't bribe. And so, Jace had fallen into a well of self-pity, and Brandon Carlisle had moved up the ranks to become chief.

Jace unclenched hands that had fisted at the thought.

It was what came after that he'd have handled differently. He rubbed his eyes, not from exhaustion this time, but to fight back the tears that threatened each time he thought of Jennifer.

"I'm pretty sure no one but my agent knows about

the cabin. I was adamant when my agent purchased it for me that no one else was to know I had any connection to it." She unlocked the front door and turned back toward the flowerpot.

He caught her hand, plucked the key from it and shoved it into his pocket. "Why would your agent buy you a cabin?"

Her delicate shoulder lifted in a shrug and she shot him a glare. "It was a mutually beneficial business arrangement. I wanted a place I could lose myself and be left alone in, and he got to enjoy weekends away with his friends, hunting, fishing, whatever else they do up here."

He couldn't blame her. The other cops had given her a rough time—a really rough time—throughout the entire investigation, but he had stayed out of it, even though, at that time, he'd still believed her ex was innocent.

"I gave Ron the money, and he bought it in his name. He gets the tax write-off and can use the cabin whenever he wants."

"Sounds like a win-win for him."

"It was worth it."

"He won't show up, will he?"

"No. He's not due to come up again for a few weeks, at least."

"Will he figure you came here?"

She shrugged. "I doubt it. But even if he does, I don't think he'll tell anyone. It would only hurt him, since I have a signed agreement with him stating the terms of the arrangement. It says very clearly that if he reveals the details of our arrangement to anyone, the deal is off, and the cabin is mine."

He wasn't about to argue with her, so he let the matter drop. He waited for Phoenix to enter, then closed and locked the door behind them. "No dead bolt?"

"No need."

Before now. She didn't add it, but he could read the hesitation in her eyes.

"Don't worry about it." Phoenix would alert him if anyone approached the cabin. He started to stretch, but the stabbing pain in his side stopped him. "Do you have a first aid kit here?"

"In the kitchen."

He followed her past a huge pit couch covered in throw pillows that took up most of the living room. He ignored the longing to lie down and close his eyes and maybe crawl beneath one of the soft-looking blankets she'd thrown over the back. He tore his attention from the couch before the urge overwhelmed him and he gave in.

An archway opened to a cozy, rustic kitchen.

Addison grabbed a bowl from a bottom cabinet, filled it with water and set it on the floor for Phoenix. "Here you go, boy." She petted his head before turning to Jace.

"Why don't you sit down?" She gestured to one of the four high-backed barstools pushed beneath a breakfast bar, then pulled open a small wood cabinet above the stainless steel refrigerator. Standing on her tiptoes, she stretched to reach into the cabinet. Her pajama shirt rode up, revealing a long, thin scar across her lower back.

Jace averted his gaze when she started to turn with the first aid kit. He pulled one of the stools from beneath the counter, slid his windbreaker off, hung it over the back of the stool and perched on the edge. Careful to pry his T-shirt from the dried blood first, he slowly rolled it up past the gouge in his side.

Addison gasped. She pressed a hand to her mouth as her face paled and she swayed a little. "Oh…"

"Are you okay?" He stood, unsure whether to reach for her or give her a minute to get her bearings.

Grabbing the counter, she steadied herself. "Yes. I'm sorry, I…I just didn't realize how badly you were injured… How did that happen?"

"I was hit while we were running."

"Hit?" Her eyes widened.

He'd never seen eyes like hers. Jade with a burst of gold surrounding the pupils.

"Shot? You were shot?"

"It's not that bad." He held out a hand for the first aid kit. "Is there a bathroom down here?"

Sucking in a deep, shaky breath, she shook her head. "I'll help you."

"I can—"

"Follow me." She turned with the first aid kit and left the room without looking back.

With no real choice, he followed her to a large bathroom at the top of the stairs.

She set the first aid kit on the counter, but didn't shift to face him. "Do you want to take a shower first?"

He definitely wanted a shower, and the oversize walk-in shower stall with multiple showerheads was extremely inviting, but he wasn't leaving her alone. Not with that skittish look in her eyes. She might just bolt if he gave her the chance. Not that he blamed her. She had to be terrified. Of course, he could cuff her again, but he had a feeling that wouldn't go over too well. Besides, he couldn't be 100 percent sure their pursuer couldn't find them, so no way could he leave her alone and unprotected. "Not right now, thanks."

She shot him a scowl.

He couldn't help the small bit of laughter that escaped. "I'll just clean up in the sink."

She held his gaze a moment longer than necessary. "There are washcloths and towels in the tall cabinet. I'll go see if Ron has a shirt that'll fit you."

Her footsteps receded down the hallway. He listened to be sure she didn't go downstairs before he grabbed a washcloth and turned on the water. He clenched his teeth and started to clean the wound. The last thing he needed was an infection. At least he didn't have to dig a bullet out. Thankfully, it had only grazed his side, though that didn't lessen the pain. When he got his hands on Connor—

Connor should have given him more information when he'd called, shouldn't have let him go in blind. Thankfully, he'd been able to get Addison to safety, but that didn't change the fact things could have gone much differently.

"Here. This should fit." She hung a light blue, long-sleeved T-shirt over the towel rack and opened the first aid kit. "Ron is quite a bit shorter than you, so his jeans won't fit, but the shirt should work okay if you push the sleeves up."

"Thanks."

She handed him a towel, and he patted his side dry while she opened a couple of bandages and tape, then held up a bottle of something. She soaked a gauze pad with the liquid from the bottle. "Stay still. This might sting."

"Agh…" He clamped his teeth tight, biting back the scream.

"Sorry." She winced and spread the bandages over the wound, her hands shaking. "Hold this."

He held the bandages in place while she smoothed tape along the edges. Her featherlight touch sent a shiver through him. He averted his gaze. It had definitely been too long since he'd been in the company of a beautiful woman. Or any woman. Or anyone, for that matter, unless you counted the customers at the clubs he provided security for, which he didn't, since he didn't interact with them.

And he planned to keep it that way. As soon as Connor showed up, he'd be out of there. After he'd failed to keep Jennifer safe, no way would he ever get involved with another woman, especially another woman he might not be able to protect. He couldn't live with two deaths on his conscience. One was enough to batter him for a lifetime.

"Would you like a couple of ibuprofen?" She held out a bottle from the first aid kit. "I'm sorry I don't have anything stronger."

"Thanks." He shook three caplets into his hand and handed back the bottle, barely resisting the urge to tame her tangled mess of hair behind her ear. Keeping himself from reaching out to comfort her was getting harder. He shoved the small glimmer of attraction aside. This woman was nothing but trouble. She was definitely off-limits, even if he was looking for a relationship, which he wasn't. If he wasn't exhausted, in pain and aggravated, he'd never even have noticed her delicate features or those big green eyes so filled with strength and determination. Despite any other feelings he might have harbored from the past, her courage touched him.

"What time will Connor be here?"

The question ripped him from his reverie. "He said they'd get here sometime after six."

Her eyes widened. "They?"

"I assume him and Maris." He shrugged. "But I didn't ask."

She caught her lower lip between her teeth as the color drained from her face.

"Is there a problem?"

"I'm going to take a shower." She shot him a pointed gaze. "I'll meet you downstairs when I'm done."

Jace watched her go. Clearly, she didn't trust him, but what could he do to change that? And why did he so badly want to?

FOUR

Addison pulled on her softest, highly faded, beat-up jeans and a hunter green sweater, the need for comfort and familiarity outweighing everything else. A hot shower and two more ibuprofen had helped ease some of the tension from her muscles, but exhaustion still weighed heavily. She toweled her hair dry, ignoring the blow-dryer, even though it would mean having to tame a mass of waves and frizz later. She'd already wasted enough time—and conditioner—in the shower trying to comb through the tangled mess. More pressing problems demanded her attention.

She tossed the towel onto a small dresser in the walk-in-closet, slid the dresser aside and opened the safe. Addison never left the house without her laptop, but she knew that in the event of an emergency, it might not always be possible to keep it with her. Thankfully, she was fanatical about backing up her work and could access it from anywhere. She pulled out the slim black laptop case, locked the safe and returned the dresser to its previous position. Satisfied no one, not even Ron, could see any part of the safe built into the closet wall, which hid not only her laptop but a small amount of

cash and the agreement she and Ron had signed, she
turned and headed downstairs with her spare laptop.

The scent of bacon hit her before she left the landing. She pressed a hand to her growling stomach as she
strode toward the kitchen.

"There you are. I was getting ready to come check
on you." Jace turned from the stove, fork in hand.

She stopped short in the doorway. "What are you
doing?"

He looked at the pan on the stove, then back at her
and lifted a brow. "Making breakfast. Hungry?"

Her traitorous stomach growled again, and she
frowned, the sight of him moving so comfortably
around her kitchen making her uneasy. "Starved, actually."

He laid the fork on a spoon rest and pulled a chair
from the table where he'd already set two places, then
gestured toward her laptop. "If you plan on working,
why don't you set it aside for now and sit?"

"I have to…um…" The need to check her email hammered her, but she wasn't ready to share that with him,
not until she knew what awaited her. If past experience
was any indication, she'd need at least a few minutes to
come to terms with whatever awaited her before she'd
be able to discuss it with anyone. Giving in to her hunger, she sat and pulled the chair in. The email could
wait a few more minutes. "Thanks."

"I found bacon in the freezer and a box of ready-mix
pancakes in the pantry, so that's the best I could do. But
there's coffee." He grinned and filled the mug he'd already placed on the table.

Spooning French vanilla–flavored powdered creamer
into her mug, she worked to steady her shaky hands.
She'd kept the cabin fairly well stocked since buying it,

just in case she needed to disappear for a while. "I'm sorry, I don't have any dog food."

Phoenix lay sleeping beside the back door, seemingly content.

"No problem. I already fed him a couple of cups of dog food I'd tossed into a small bag in case we were gone longer than expected. Connor was pretty vague when he first called."

She nodded, still not ready to deal with Connor. Or Maris. Though she was going to have to think about her sister sometime, probably soon.

If only Maris had come to Addison, at least warned her before writing the article accusing Brandon of a multitude of illegal activities and of having numerous affairs, things might have been different. If Addison hadn't found out about his crimes and indiscretions along with the rest of the world, maybe she'd have been more able to understand, more prepared to forgive.

Would it really have mattered, though? Would Addison have believed her if Maris had come to her? Was her anger at Maris really because she hadn't asked Addison's permission or given her a heads-up before writing her article? Or was it the fact that she'd shattered Addison's illusions, destroyed her relationship with her husband—a relationship that had apparently existed only in Addison's mind and heart—and sent her world crashing into ruins?

It didn't matter. Although Addison had come to believe every last word Maris had written about him, Maris hadn't had enough proof, and Brandon had walked away a free man. But Maris hadn't stopped with Brandon. She'd implicated a number of his associates, as well, Jace included.

Addison had struggled to forgive her sister for years,

despite knowing in her heart that it was the right thing to do. On some level, she supposed she had forgiven her, mostly, though the pain Maris had caused wasn't easy to forget.

She shoved thoughts of the past away. She had enough to worry about in the present. "How's your side?"

Jace shrugged and flipped the pancakes. "I'll live."

Abruptly running out of conversation, Addison sipped her coffee before pulling the charger and computer from the bag. She plugged it in and set it up on the table beside her.

"When you said a cabin in the mountains, I have to admit, this isn't what I pictured." He grinned, a sparkle lighting his blue eyes. Something about his smile was contagious—maybe the dimple denting his right cheek—and she couldn't help but join him.

"I wanted something cozy." The two-bedroom cabin definitely fit the bill. She'd spent many nights tucked away here, the living room fireplace fighting back the cold, bringing a sense of serenity that had eluded her over most of the past few years. She signed into her email, then shifted the computer aside as Jace placed a serving platter in the center of the table.

"Dig in." He sat across from her and pulled his chair closer to the table, then forked three pancakes onto his plate and added syrup.

She watched him.

He frowned, a forkful of pancake stopping halfway to his mouth. "Don't you like pancakes?"

She shook her head.

He lowered his fork to his plate and slid his chair back. "I can make you something else."

"No, it's not that. I mean… I like pancakes just fine.

It's just…well…" She shook her head again, not really knowing where to go with him. She didn't trust him. How could she, when there was a chance he'd been involved in any illegal activities with her ex? How could she trust anyone, when the one person she had trusted had hidden his true nature from her throughout their entire marriage?

She propped her elbows on the table and pressed the heels of her hands into her eyes. Crying wouldn't help anything.

And to be honest, Jace had never harassed her, as the other cops had. She'd have remembered him instantly if he had.

Maybe Brandon had fooled Jace just as much as he'd fooled her, and maybe Maris had been wrong about him. What did the Bible say? *Judge not, and you will not be judged; condemn not, and you will not be condemned; forgive, and you will be forgiven.*

She blew out a breath and folded her arms on the table. She'd do well to remember those lessons, not only pertaining to Jace, but to Maris, too. "If he stays true to the time line in the book, I only have a week to find him."

"Whoa." He held his hands up, palms toward her in a gesture of surrender. "What do you mean *I*?"

Heat blossomed in her cheeks. "I meant I only have one week to find him before he kills someone else."

"You can't possibly think you're going searching for a killer on your own."

She caught his gaze and held it. "Don't you get it? I can't be responsible for another murder. I can't stand the thought of another woman dying because I chose her, because I brought her to the attention of some serial killer."

"Addison, you're not responsible for the actions of a killer."

"Aren't I?"

Jace raked a hand through his hair in what was becoming a familiar gesture. He opened his mouth, as if to say something, then closed it again and studied her.

She shoved her empty plate away, the roiling in her stomach no longer from hunger, and pulled the laptop closer. Ignoring him, she opened her email. Over a hundred new messages since she'd last checked. She skimmed through the subject lines, knowing exactly what she was looking for, and found it halfway through the list. She squeezed her eyes shut and prayed she was wrong. The familiar words—*The Final Victim*—floated in her mind. The few sips of coffee she'd swallowed threatened to come back up.

"What are you doing?"

Her hand shook convulsively as she lifted the coffee cup to her mouth just so she'd have something to do, something to distract her from the new message glaring at her from the screen. Coffee sloshed over the side of the mug and onto the table. She lowered it without taking a sip. No way she'd get it past the lump in her throat anyway. "Working on something."

"Listen, Addison, I know you've had your problems with the police, and Connor was very clear that I shouldn't involve them, but once he gets here…"

She snorted, the sound not very ladylike, but it summed up her feelings for the police.

"There are probably still some good men on the force…" Something about the statement seemed off, as if he was trying to convince himself as much as her. "Besides, no one wants a killer on the loose. Even the crooked cops will work to stop him."

"Really? And how do you know that? Because *you* would have tried to stop him?" She slammed the computer closed, fully aware she was being a class A jerk—even after he'd gone through the trouble of making breakfast and coffee...and saving her life—but unable to stop herself. Her emotions were too all over the place, bubbling up within her with nowhere to go, no way to vent.

She yanked the charger from the socket and rolled it loosely before picking up the computer. With the thought of opening the newest email from the killer hammering her relentlessly, she stormed out of the kitchen. Barely checking the urge to slam the computer onto her desk, she dropped into the comfortable desk chair in the corner of the living room. The chair was still new enough that the smell of leather enveloped her, bringing an odd, unexpected wave of comfort. If she could think clearly, maybe she could figure this out.

Sighing, she took a moment to massage her pounding temples, then plugged the computer in, opened it and returned to the dreaded email. With the sounds of dishes clattering in the sink, water running and cabinets opening and closing as background music, she clicked on the subject line marked *The Final Victim*.

She closed her eyes, breathing deeply, and counted to ten. Okay. She could do this. She braced herself, opened her eyes and read the one-line message.

The game is on.

"What does that mean?"

She screamed and jumped from the chair, smacking the top of her head on Jace's chin.

"Ouch." He scowled and rubbed his jaw.

Holding her head, she glared at him. "What is wrong with you?"

"Me?"

"How could you sneak up on me like that? You scared me nearly to death." She leaned a hip against the desk and held a hand to her chest, hoping to keep her heart from jumping out, and shot him a scowl. "Why are you looking over my shoulder, anyway?"

"I promised Connor I'd keep you alive until he got here."

She took a deep, shaky breath and let it out slowly. "Please, could I have a few minutes alone?"

He propped his hands low on his hips. He hadn't shaved, and the stubble darkening his cheeks, combined with the hardness in his eyes, gave him a dangerous appearance. "Sure thing."

Her computer screen went dark, pulling her attention back to the problem at hand. She sat and scooted her chair in, trying to regain her composure as she lit the screen back up. The message had come from another unfamiliar email address, different from the first two. Only four words. The game is on. Four words that held the power to destroy her. She closed the message and scrolled through the rest of her inbox. Several messages from Ron, even more from her publicist. She ignored them. She'd answer them later when she could think more clearly. Right now, a more pressing matter needed her attention.

"What are you doing?" Her voice shook.

Jace stood in front of a bookshelf, one of two that lined the walls on either side of the stone fireplace, scanning titles on the spines of what had to be close to a hundred books. "Looking for something."

"I just wanted to say I'm sorry."

"You have nothing to be sorry for." He couldn't imagine what kind of pain she must be dealing with.

"I snapped at you, and I didn't mean to."

Giving up on the books for a moment, he turned to face her. "First off, I startled you, and I'm sorry for that. I don't blame you for snapping. And second, well, you're dealing with a lot right now. I just hope you'll begin to trust me at some point."

She lowered her gaze.

Sooner or later, he'd gain her confidence, but for now, he returned his attention to the shelves. *The Final Victim.* Ah…bingo. Alphabetized by author, just like the rest of the books. He pulled out the hardcover copy and flipped to chapter one.

"You're going to read my book?" She lifted a skeptical brow.

"I need answers. Who knows? Maybe they're in here somewhere." Taking the book with him, he flopped onto the couch, facing the wall of windows overlooking the yard, and propped his feet on one of the ottomans in the center of the pit.

She sighed and perched on the edge of the couch, choosing a corner as far from him as possible, looking ready to bolt with the slightest provocation. "Why do you need answers if you're going to walk away as soon as Connor gets here to relieve you?"

Good question. Too bad he didn't have an answer. "Curiosity. What can I say? I love a good whodunit."

People were dying. How could she think he wouldn't at least try to help? What did she take him for? Oh, right, a criminal. She'd already made that clear. Hadn't she ever heard, *Judge not lest ye be judged*? She had no idea what he'd been through, no idea what doing the right thing had cost him—

First, his career, when Maris's article had hit the stands and he'd finally realized what his partner was doing. He'd tried to do the right thing, and cooperated fully with Internal Affairs, but he hadn't known anything, therefore had no proof. With no one to back him up, he'd failed miserably, giving Brandon the opportunity to set him up to take the fall. And Jace had been left with no choice but to resign.

His self-respect was another casualty, when he'd turned to alcohol rather than God to alleviate his anger and resentment.

The worst thing about it all was losing Jennifer, a woman he'd vowed to honor, love and protect. Jennifer had been killed in their apartment by an intruder who was never caught, though he suspected Brandon had a hand in her death. But at the end of the day, that was no one's fault but his own. If he'd gone straight home that night, rather than stopping off at the bar for a few drinks that had turned into more than a few while he spent over an hour wallowing in self-pity, he'd have made it home before she died. The coroner's report had proven that the time of death was only half an hour before he'd walked in. Could he have saved her? Maybe. And maybe not. But he'd never know, because he'd been too busy feeling sorry for himself to go home to the wife who'd stood by his side through everything, who'd believed in him, who'd trusted him. Obviously, her trust had been misplaced.

And now here was Addison. Was she his chance at redemption? An opportunity to atone for at least some of his sins? He'd already made his peace with God, after finding Phoenix on his doorstep and being given the chance to take care of another being despite how badly he'd failed. Had God placed him in Addison's life to help save her from this killer? How could he walk away without finding out?

Besides, somehow Connor was involved in all of this, and no matter what their differences—traitor or not—the man was still like a brother. Just a long-lost brother he didn't talk to anymore.

"Fine." She held his gaze a moment longer. "Ask whatever you want to know."

He lowered the book to his lap, keeping it open to the first page. "Okay. Let's start with the email I saw on your computer. The game is on. That's the first phrase I planned on skimming through the book for, because I have a sneaking suspicion I'll find those exact words in here. Probably fairly close to the beginning of the story."

She pulled her knees to her chest, curling into the corner. Her brow furrowed. "The killer sends the lead detective a note after the second murder. 'The game is on.' She doesn't understand it at first."

He sat forward and rested his elbows on his knees, his interest piqued. "But you do?"

"Like I told you earlier, it's all a game to him—a head game with the lead detective. But the stakes are life and death." She hugged one of the many throw pillows close to her. "Over time, the killer lays out the rules. One rule after each murder."

"Okay. So you have the advantage."

She shook her head and frowned at him as if he'd lost his mind. "How do you figure?"

"Theoretically, you already know all the rules. You don't have to wait for another murder."

"I don't understand how that helps."

He shifted to ease some of the pain in his side and

to keep his waistband from rubbing against the bandaged wound. "Tell me more about the game. How does someone win?"

"I told you before—they live."

"Elaborate."

"The winner lives. The game doesn't end until one of them dies."

"Does he have a death wish?"

"No. He thinks if he kills the lead detective, he'll be able to stop killing because he'd have won."

"He won't, I take it?"

She shot him a look. "Of course not. He's just telling himself that. He tries to kill her several times throughout the book. The first attempt is right after the second murder, before he sends the note telling her about the game. Because she was able to elude him, he viewed her as a worthy adversary and started giving her rules. Clues, kind of."

"Let me guess, he breaks into her house and tries to shoot her."

"No, actually." She frowned. "He tries to run her down with his car, but her partner pushes her out of the way. Odd, don't you think, that he'd deviate from the story there when he stuck so rigidly to the murder scenes?"

"Maybe not. He had a lot of time to plan and control the murder scenes. He couldn't be sure he could get you where he needed to follow the story line when he came after you. Plus, someone did try to run us off the road. The killer? Probably. What kind of car did he drive in the book?"

"A silver…" She paled. "Sedan. I didn't give a make or model."

"Just like the one that tried to run us off the road.

Who knows? Maybe he never meant to kill you when he broke into your house last night but planned to flush you out, chase you into the night so he could run you down." He didn't know what to make of that, or where to go from there, so he put it aside for the moment after making a mental note to check car rentals in the area around Addison's house. He doubted the killer would have bought the car, but if he did, they'd need an entire team of experts to hunt down every silver sedan sold on Long Island and in the surrounding areas. "So, theoretically, either the lead detective or the killer will be the final victim. Or, in this case, you or the killer, since he seems to have cast you in the lead detective's role."

She nodded but didn't elaborate.

He changed tactics. No need to make her any more frightened than she already was. "Do you have a pen and paper?"

She got up and went to her desk.

He closed his eyes, just for a minute, to ease some of the strain. The puzzle pieces tumbled through his mind, rearranging themselves over and over in search of the way they best fit together. If he was honest with himself, he had to admit that having a puzzle to solve again felt good. It stimulated something in him that had been too long dormant. It had been a long time since he'd applied his mind to a problem. He'd had a good amount of savings, and after resigning from the force and losing Jennifer, he'd supplemented it by taking odd jobs here and there, most often as a bouncer at some club or another, where liquor had been readily available.

"Here."

He jumped, startled and rubbed the sleepiness from his eyes.

She held out a spiral notebook and pen.

"Oh, thanks." Sliding forward, he dropped the notebook onto the ottoman, opened it and leaned over. "I need to know everything you can tell me about each of the victims in the book. We'll see if we can narrow any of them down. If we can figure out who he's going to kill ahead of time, maybe we can stop it. Is there anyone in particular you can think of who matches the description of one of the victims?"

She caught her lower lip between her teeth and nodded but made no move to sit. "Only the last person he kills in book one…"

"The detective's sister?"

She nodded and paced between the couch and the fireplace a few times, one arm crossed tightly over her stomach while she chewed on the thumbnail of the other hand.

No wonder Connor was in such a panic.

Jace had spent the last five years loathing Maris, the woman who'd ruined his life, destroyed his career and stolen his best friend, all because she'd written a story without being 100 percent certain her facts were accurate, with absolutely no regard for whom she might hurt. He'd searched his heart for forgiveness and come up short time and time again. And now he had already taken a bullet to protect her sister.

Maybe God was tired of waiting for him to do the right thing and had given him a nudge in the right direction, despite the fact he'd lost faith for some time and turned to alcohol instead. Jace could take a lesson in forgiveness.

"So the title *The Final Victim* isn't actually referring to the last woman he kills but to whomever loses the game the killer is playing."

She nodded again.

"Okay. How many people die in the book? Five, you said?"

"Yes." She curled back into the corner of the couch and closed her eyes. After a few minutes, her breathing evened out, and he thought exhaustion might finally have claimed her. When she spoke, her voice was racked with pain. "How do you forgive yourself when you feel responsible for the death of another?"

If only he could answer that question.

FIVE

Jace still sat on the couch, where he'd spent the entire afternoon immersed in her book, scribbling frantically in the notebook he'd already half filled.

Phoenix lay on the floor at Jace's feet. He lifted his head and cocked it to the side, studying her.

She'd always wanted a dog, but Brandon had been adamant. No animals in the house. She should have gotten one right away after she moved out, had even thought of getting one for companionship and protection, but decided against it. If Brandon found out about it, he'd have found a way to take it from her. She didn't want to risk an innocent animal getting hurt. Seemed she was doomed to a life devoid of love.

She glanced at Jace, and for just an instant, the thought of him as something more flashed into her head. She squashed it before it could fully form. If Brandon would have taken a dog from her, she couldn't even imagine what he'd do if she tried to have any kind of relationship with another man, a good man, a man she might be able to trust, to confide in, to share her life with. Was Jace all of those things? He'd come in the middle of the night to save her at Connor's request, no questions asked, even though there were obviously issues there. Did that make him a good person? Dependable, for sure, but good? Maybe—if his association with Brandon really had been as innocent…and naive…as her own. Jace didn't strike her as naive. Either way, now certainly wasn't the time to pursue her interest in finding out.

"Do you want coffee?"

Jace jerked his head up. "I'm sorry?"

She couldn't help the small surge of satisfaction. He'd obviously been fully engrossed in her story. Either that, or he'd fallen asleep while reading. "I'm going to make coffee. Would you like some?"

He turned her book over on the table and frowned. "What time is it?"

"Around two, maybe two thirty."

He pulled his cell phone from his pocket and checked the screen.

"You won't get good service up here. I have satellite internet, which is slow enough, but the cell phone service is spotty at best."

He rubbed a hand over his heavy five-o'clock shadow. "We're going to have to go into town. I used the last of the coffee this morning, and I need more dog food, anyway." He stood from the couch and winced, favoring his injured side. "Phoenix, come."

"We're going now?"

The big dog trotted to his side. "May as well. I have to check for messages, anyway, see if Connor called. I'm just going to check the yard with Phoenix, then we'll go. I'll be right back."

She dropped into the desk chair, where she'd spent most of the afternoon staring at a blank screen and thinking, then opened a dialogue box. Ron usually kept his instant messaging open when he was in the office. Hey Ron, you around?

His response popped up almost immediately. Is something wrong?

He had to be kidding. She refrained from any smart remarks. I was thinking...

Now to find a tactful way to phrase her request so as not to send him into a snit. She lowered her gaze to the pristine keyboard, missing the quirks of the laptop she usually used, and clasped her hands over the back of her head. Did she really want to do this? She'd worked so hard on these books, invested years during her marriage, while her husband was running around with other women and engaging in a myriad of illegal activities. Maybe if she'd emerged from the writing cave now and then, she'd have seen what was going on without Maris having to shove it under her nose. But probably not. Writing was one of the few escapes Brandon had allowed her during the years she'd been chained to him, though he'd put his foot down about writing romance. Brandon Carlisle didn't come second to any man, not even a fictional one.

The ding of a new message pulled her focus back to her current dilemma. You still there?

Blowing out a breath, she started typing before she could change her mind. See if my pub will pull the books.

WHAT?! Are you crazy?

An image of him, red-faced and fully focused on his computer screen, jumped into her head. Oh, well. There was no other choice. He'd have to get over it.

I want them to pull the book and delay or cancel the release of book 2. I'll pay back the advance, including your commission.

Though it would mean selling the cabin she'd come to love. No matter. She stood and stretched her back. If she knew Ron, which she did, it would take him a little while to respond. He'd carefully craft and recraft his response for maximum impact, to make her see things reasonably. It wouldn't work. She didn't feel like being reasonable. She was trapped in a cabin in the middle of nowhere, unable to contact anyone—although who she'd contact if she could was beyond her.

Her parents were long gone, both having died when she was a child, and it had been years since she'd spoken to her only sister, whose father had raised her after her mother's death but hadn't ever really loved her. And Brandon had made her cut ties with any friends she'd had soon after they were married. By the time the divorce was final, Addison no longer trusted anyone enough to pursue friendships. And now it seemed her writing was being taken from her, as well. The one thing that had kept her sane through her marriage, her divorce, the investigation…

The screen went black, pulling her from her pity party. Leaving it open, she turned away. Maybe Ron was contacting the powers that be in an effort to honor her request. She sighed and stood. Probably not.

Jace pulled the car as close to the front steps as he could and left the passenger door open, then left Phoenix in the back seat and jogged up the front steps. "Get in quickly."

As she ran down the few steps to the car, Jace locked the cabin door and followed closely behind.

Once they were all in the car with the doors locked, Addison turned and clipped the seat belt to Phoenix's harness, then snapped her own seat belt shut. She didn't know how much longer she could live on the run, constantly looking over her shoulder, in fear not only for her life, but the lives of those around her.

Jace checked the rearview mirror, then swung the vehicle back, turned around and headed down the driveway. "It's a good book."

A small smile tugged at her. She wrestled down the urge to ask if he'd finished it, what his favorite part was, if he liked the characters, and a hundred other questions her self-doubt begged her to ask. "Thank you."

He frowned.

All her insecurities flooded to the surface. "What?"

Instead of answering, he lowered the visor against the bright afternoon sun, looked up and down the deserted road, then finally pulled out. After an endless moment of silence, where she mentally rewrote every scene she'd ever had doubts about, he finally glanced at her before returning his attention to the road ahead of him…and the road behind him, and the woods bordering them on both sides. How could he possibly keep his attention so split, yet seem so fully focused on everything?

"It's a complex story, a number of characters, plenty of suspects, enough suspense to keep you interested."

Her mouth dropped open. Somehow, she hadn't expected such an in-depth critique from him. Maybe it was the gruff exterior, the rugged strength he exuded without even seeming to realize it.

He massaged his neck and tilted his head back, then straightened. "But I'm not sure how it helps us. Other than similar appearances, the victims don't have much, if anything, in common. They don't share the same activities or lifestyles, don't frequent the same businesses, don't share a common interest or hobby, don't even live in the same neighborhoods or run in the same social circles. How does he choose them? It seems almost random. I haven't gotten all the way through the book, but there has to be some kind of common thread."

Caught off guard by the comment, Addison hesitated. She'd written a synopsis for the third book for her editor but hadn't worked out all of the more intricate details yet. "I haven't decided yet. I've created extensive backstories and motivations for a number of characters, each of them having not only motive but opportunity and a grudge against the detective, and each of them having crossed paths with the victims at some point. Any one of them could be the killer. That way, the red herrings would seem believable and readers could enjoy trying to solve the puzzle along with the detective. I didn't want to make a final decision on who the killer is until I reach that point in the writing, but you have to remember, his main motive is revenge against the lead detective. The women he chooses are secondary."

"Didn't you already write book two? Doesn't he get caught in the second book?"

"Book two is written and with my editor but hasn't been released yet." Addison offered a half smile. "And no, he doesn't get caught in book two, either."

"No?"

"No." She glanced over her shoulder. No one behind them. Yet. That had to be a good sign. The urge to flee back to the cabin and hide almost overwhelmed her, and had she been alone, she would probably have done just that, but Phoenix needed to be cared for.

Jace stared at her, his expression unreadable.

"It's a trilogy."

"Does he get caught in the third book?"

"I don't know. Probably." When she'd written the proposal for the trilogy, she'd included his capture and death in book three, when he would become *The Final Victim.* But as she'd finished writing and then editing book two, she'd considered letting him get away in hopes of prolonging the series. At the time, she'd decided to wait and see how book two sold before approaching her editor with the suggestion.

"I don't understand how you can write three books where the same killer keeps escaping."

"Why not? A lot of authors do it. Besides..." She leaned close and lowered her voice to a stage whisper. "News flash. Sometimes, even in real life, the bad guy gets away."

He shrugged. "I guess I'm not that into cliff-hangers. I like a clean ending. All the pieces tied up nice and neat."

If she hadn't been looking right at him, she'd have missed his jaw tightening, the flash of pain in his eyes. "I guess you have some experience with the bad guy getting away?"

He was quiet so long she didn't think he'd answer, then he sighed and spoke quietly. "My wife, Jennifer."

Why the sudden stab of pain in her heart at his mention of a wife? She ignored it. It didn't matter.

"She was killed, and her killer got away."

"Oh, Jace, I'm so very sorry." The pain around her heart increased, squeezing, robbing her of breath.

He nodded, his jaw clenched tight.

"How long ago?"

"Almost four years, now."

Right around the time of Brandon's investigation.

Surely Jace must have investigated his wife's murder, even with everything else going on? He seemed like the kind of man who'd have made that a priority. "Do you have any leads?"

He rolled his shoulders, tilted his head back and forth. A quick glance in his side mirror brought a frown.

Addison looked behind them at the blur of passing trees on either side but didn't see anything.

"No, no leads, once I pulled myself out of a bottle long enough to investigate." Disgust twisted his features. "I developed a drinking problem during the mess with Brandon. Had I not, I might have been able to save Jennifer."

"I'm sure it wasn't your fault," she said quietly, unsure what else to say, yet wanting so badly to offer comfort.

"I'm sorry." Guilt poured off him in waves. "I can't… I just can't talk about it."

"Oh, no, I'm sorry." She laid a hand on his arm. "I didn't mean to pry."

He looked down at her hand but didn't shake it off. "No, it's okay. It's just… I haven't spoken with anyone about it, pulled away from everyone I knew at the time. I'm pretty sure Jennifer's death had something to do with Brandon, though I haven't been able to prove it. To be honest, I just didn't know who I could trust. So I trusted no one. Not even Connor, who had been a brother to me my whole life."

She squeezed his arm, then lowered her hand to her lap. She could certainly understand why he hadn't trusted anyone. Hadn't she done the same thing? "What happened between you and Connor?"

He shrugged. "Connor and I lived next door to each other when we were kids, and we were the best of friends, inseparable. When I was sixteen, my parents were killed, murdered by a street thug for whatever little bit of cash my dad had in his pocket—cash he'd have handed over if the man had only asked. Instead, he killed them, searched my dad's pockets, grabbed my mother's purse and ran. Connor's family took me in, and we became brothers in every sense of the word."

"Did they catch the man who killed your parents?"

"No. Despite the security camera footage of the attack, the man got away."

Addison closed her eyes and inhaled deeply, past the lump in her throat. No wonder he liked nice, clean endings. He'd suffered enough cliff-hangers to last a lifetime.

"So I decided then and there that I'd be a police officer, help people, make sure nothing like that happened to another child's family." He scoffed. "And look how that turned out."

"Thanks to Brandon Carlisle. And Maris's story." Because she had no doubt now. Maris had been wrong about him. No way had Jace been involved in Brandon's crimes. "I don't—"

A loud pop cut her off.

The car's back end swung around, and Jace wrestled the wheel. "Down!"

Phoenix followed the command, instantly dropping to lie on the back seat.

Addison slid down as much as she could, bracing herself and keeping her head low. "What's happening?"

"Someone shot out the tire." Jace hit the unlock button as he skidded to a stop on the shoulder. He reached across her and swung the passenger door open. "Go. Stay low."

Addison released her seat belt and slid from the car, then shoved the front seat forward, crawled in and released Phoenix's belt.

Jace scanned the ridge while he waited. He'd seen the flash from high on the left side of the road, a small outcropping of rocks. It would take the killer time to scramble over and come after them, but not that much time.

As soon as Addison had Phoenix out and crouching beside the back tire, he half climbed, half dove over the center console and passenger seat and onto the ground. Using the open passenger door as cover, he pulled his weapon and searched the road and shoulder. No one. "Go. Into the trees."

"But—"

"I'm right behind you. Go!"

Keeping low, Addison ran.

Jace kept his gun trained on a small opening in the trees, the spot the killer would most likely emerge from if he took a direct route from the rocks.

Phoenix whined at his side.

"Quiet, boy," he whispered, knowing Phoenix would understand the command.

The big dog went on alert, his ears perked up, hackles raised.

As soon as Addison crossed into the tree line, he followed with Phoenix at his side. He entered the woods exactly where she had and found her using a tree trunk as cover, her eyes wide, and a thick, long-dead branch clutched against her chest in a white-knuckled grip. He bit back a grin. No time.

"Now what?" Her teeth chattered as she waited.

With the front tire blown out and the rim most likely bent from his wrestling the car under control and onto the shoulder, the car was useless.

Connor had been adamant—no police, though Brandon Carlisle's reach was most likely limited to the SCPD and maybe the surrounding areas. Jace doubted he would have any influence over a department all the way in upstate New York in a small town like Shady Creek. Of course, Connor hadn't known they'd have to run, either. Still, even if he did call 911, they couldn't wait like sitting ducks for the cops to get there.

A shot ricocheted off a nearby tree, forcing his hand.

"Go," he whispered and gestured deeper into the woods. "Slow. Quiet."

Addison nodded, slipping into the brush.

Phoenix followed her.

Jace backed up with them. If only he could get a glimpse of the guy, maybe take him out before they had to run.

Another shot rang out.

The guy was good at camouflage, he'd give him that.

"Will the game end now, Addison?" The killer's laughter echoed through the forest.

Unable to pinpoint his location, Jace continued to back up with Addison and Phoenix, covering them as they retreated. The killer had made it to this side of the road, that much he could tell. Could the guy track? Jace didn't know, but had to assume he could.

"Are you ready to become the final victim?" the man taunted. "If you do, no one else will die."

Jace whirled just as Addison peeked from behind the cover of the tree behind him.

A bullet whizzed past his ear.

She clutched her shoulder and went down.

Jace scrambled through the brush, covered her body with his. Now what? Pinned down by a killer, Addison injured—no clue how badly—and nowhere to retreat, except deeper into the forest, if Addison could move. "How bad?"

"I'm okay," she hissed through clenched teeth. "Not bad, just stings."

"Okay, all right. Stay put."

"Wait." She sobbed softly and scrambled to regain the branch she'd dropped when she fell. "Where are you going?"

"It's okay. I'll be right back." He had no choice but to leave her to go after the guy. Keeping low, he crept forward, just a little.

Phoenix belly-crawled to Addison's side and lay still.

"Phoenix, stay." He pulled out his cell phone. Okay. Five bars. He dialed Connor.

"Come out, come out, or I'll come after you," the killer taunted. "I know you're not dead. Yet."

Voice mail. No further need for stealth, since Addison had already given away their position when she'd peeked from behind the tree—a decision he'd be sure to discuss with her later, once they were safe and he'd tended to her wound. Jace raised his voice, hoping the echo would keep the killer from pinpointing the exact tree he'd hidden behind. "She won't die today, but you will if you come any closer."

Silence. Jace waited, giving his opponent time to consider his options. If he was smart, he'd run. Jace dialed Connor again. Still no answer. He shifted and scanned the woods. A dark patch moved behind a thick stand of pricker bushes. Without being able to see clearly, no way could he take a shot.

"This can end now." The killer's teasing tone was gone, replaced by anger. He'd probably been watching the road, the most logical route in and out of the area, after he'd lost them the last time. Maybe he didn't realize Jace would still be with her, or that he'd be armed. Or maybe he'd cast Jace in the role of the detective's partner. Either way… "All you have to do is come out, Addison, and it'll all be over."

Tears streamed down Addison's cheeks.

From what Jace had seen of her so far, he had no doubt she'd give herself up to save the others she felt responsible for. "You said yourself the killer in your book was lying. What's to say this one isn't, too? He probably won't stop killing even if you do go out there."

She squeezed her eyes closed tight and nodded.

Jace dialed 911.

Before he could hit Call, the sounds of someone crashing through the forest in the opposite direction made him pause.

Go after him or stay with Addison and Phoenix? He lurched to his feet, barreled through the small patch of woods they'd retreated into.

A car door slammed.

Jace hit the street running.

A silver sedan shot from its hiding spot not a hundred feet down and rocketed onto the road, fishtailing as it headed straight for him.

Jace dove to the side, rolled over the hood of his own car and came up in a crouch, gun aimed steady at the retreating vehicle. Too far for a clean shot. Ugh… Frustration pounded in his head. No sense dwelling on what he couldn't change. He turned to go back to Addison.

She stood not five feet away, the thick branch she'd been clutching held over her bleeding shoulder in a firm two-handed grip. Battered, bleeding and ready to defend him and Phoenix and herself to the best of her ability. His warrior.

Yikes! Where had that come from? He shook off whatever it was that had gripped him in that instant. "Are you hurt?"

"I'm fine." She lowered the branch but didn't loosen her grip. "I don't even think the bullet hit me. I think it ricocheted and a piece of bark or something hit my shoulder."

"Still, why would you stick your head out? You told me he'd probably keep on killing even if he won."

"And I believe he would."

"Then why leave your cover?" With his adrenaline rush ebbing, anger crept in.

Her eyes went wide. "I didn't mean to get shot. I just thought maybe I could reason with him."

Jace just closed his eyes, shook his head and offered a quick prayer of thanks that she hadn't been killed and the killer had taken off. He patted Phoenix's head. "Good boy."

Phoenix licked his hand.

"So…" Addison looked up and down the deserted road, then back at the disabled car. "Now what?"

"Now you and Phoenix stay hidden while I change the tire. Then we go back to the cabin."

"What about the dog food?"

He petted Phoenix's side, pulling him close. "Looks like tonight, Phoenix gets to eat people food."

"Do you think he'll come back? The killer, I mean?"

Jace chewed it over. The last time he'd spoken, the killer had sounded angry. He'd obviously realized he'd lost that round, since he'd fled. So now what would he do? "I have no idea. What do you think?"

"Me?" She looked off in the direction the man had gone. "How would I know what he'll do next?"

He shrugged. "Give it some thought. The best way to catch a monster like this is to get in his head, which you should be able to do. Look at your killer's motivation, think about what makes him do what he does, decide how he chooses his victims. Maybe this killer is trying to mirror that as best he can without knowing the full story."

She nodded and backed to the edge of the woods, then sat.

Phoenix lay beside her and dropped his head onto her lap.

Staring off into space, keeping her branch close, she absently stroked Phoenix's head.

He'd taken a liking to her, Jace realized. Phoenix, that was, not Jace. Though he had to admit a certain amount of respect for her and maybe something more, something he wasn't ready to examine, would probably never be ready to examine. Jace left her to her thoughts and shot Connor a quick text to bring dog food and coffee.

Though he scanned the road, there was no way to tell if a sniper still crouched in the trees. He popped the trunk, took out the jack and tried to keep his attention focused everywhere as he changed the tire with a giant bull's-eye on his back.

SIX

As soon as they returned to the cabin, Jace ushered Addison inside, cleaned and bandaged her shoulder—which turned out to be nothing more than a nick—and headed out to secure the property with Phoenix, leaving Addison alone with her thoughts.

She watched through the window above the sink as Jace ran along the edge of the tree line with the big dog at his side. It would have seemed such a normal, everyday activity, if not for the scowl he wore while he continuously scanned the woods and yard, stopping every now and then to study something closer.

Tearing her gaze from the window, she took a glass of water to the living room and settled at the computer. She hit a random key to bring up the screen.

Ron's response to her earlier message waited. Let's be reasonable, Addison. I spoke to the powers that be, and we've decided to hold off for now and see what happens. Who knows? Maybe it's all a coincidence.

She closed the message box. It didn't matter. There was no guarantee pulling the book would have stopped the killer anyway. All that mattered now was finding a way to stop him from killing anyone else—from killing Maris.

Maris. She and her sister had once been so close. Massaging her temples, Addison searched for calm. How had things between them gone so wrong? Oh, right. Maris had taken it upon herself to write a story about Addison's husband without even giving her any advance warning. Apparently, a lot of the information had hit close enough to home for Brandon to think it had come from Addison. And he'd tormented her for betraying him.

She pulled up her email. There had to be a clue to who the killer was, something she'd overlooked.

She sensed Jace hovering and looked up from the list of email messages.

With one hand on the back of her chair and the other on the desk, he leaned over her right shoulder. "Anything?"

Phoenix dropped his head onto her left leg.

She twined her fingers through his shaggy coat, his warmth bringing a sense of companionship, leaving her feeling a little less alone. "No. I went through the list three times, and that was after I ran a search that came up with nothing. None of the email addresses match."

When this was all over, she was definitely getting a dog. She'd go to the shelter. Maybe the dog she rescued would also rescue her, save her from the solitude she'd been hiding in for the past five years. Who was she kidding? She'd been hiding in solitude a lot longer than five years, had hidden alone throughout most of her marriage. No, not alone. God had been with her, had helped her through the worst of her past, probably would have helped more if she had reached out more.

Phoenix glanced up, catching Addison's gaze, and tilted his head into her palm.

Who knew? Maybe there was still room in her heart

for love. If she could find a way to forgive herself for the past.

"Do you believe in God, Jace?"

He straightened and looked down into her eyes.

She wasn't sure why she'd asked, or why his answer mattered so much, but it did. Had God truly sent him to save her? Could Jace really have been the answer to her plea for help? "I'm sorry. I didn't mean to ask something so personal."

"No, it's okay. I'm just… I want to be sure I answer honestly." After another moment, he took a deep breath, then spoke quietly. "I think somewhere in my heart I always believed, but I turned away for a long time, through the Internal Affairs investigation, then losing my wife. I was so angry. It was only later…"

He moved to crouch beside Phoenix and lay a hand on the dog's head. "After I found Phoenix on my doorstep, I realized maybe God hadn't given up on me, even though I'd pretty much given up on myself. Phoenix had a collar and a tag with his name on it, so I put an ad in the local paper and in a few social media groups. When no one claimed him, I accepted God was giving me a second chance. So, I prayed for the first time in a long time, begged for forgiveness, for help, for strength, for guidance. And He answered. I was finally able to quit drinking and focus on searching for Jennifer's killer. Though I still haven't found him, I'm confident one day I will."

"Do you think you'll ever go back to the police force?"

He shrugged. "I'm not sure. I'd like to, love to, actually, but not with Brandon Carlisle and his buddies in charge. That wouldn't bode well for me."

That was certainly an understatement.

Jace returned to his spot at her side, leaning over to see the laptop screen. Apparently, their heart-to-heart had ended. "Did you open each email and check the signature lines, see if he signed them in any way, even just to taunt?"

She froze. She hadn't thought of that, couldn't even recall if there was a signature line on either of the messages from the killer. She could envision the passage from her book, and the images of the victims were seared into her brain, tormenting her every time she closed her eyes, but she couldn't recall a signature. Stupid mistake. "No."

"If he did take some sort of credit, it might give us an idea how he's thinking, and we desperately need that to get into his head."

She pulled up the first message from the killer, avoiding studying the pictures too closely, ignoring the pang of grief for the stranger who'd died by her hand, and scrolled to the bottom. Nothing. She checked the second and third emails. "No signatures."

There really was no need to tell him. He could see clearly enough from his position over her shoulder, leaning close to see the screen, heat emanating from him. A line of sweat dripped down her back. Claustrophobia overwhelmed her, the need to escape his hovering presence a physical ache.

Darkness assailed her, closing in from both sides, tunneling her vision. Walls closed in on her, squeezing. She clamped her teeth until her jaw ached, but didn't dare scream. She had to hide. Blackness threatened to suffocate her. She had to help. She had to escape the smell, the same smell as when she'd fallen and bloodied her nose. She curled into a ball, making herself smaller. She had to hide. She had to help…had to hide… to help…she had to see—"No!"

She lurched to her feet, startling the big dog from her lap and toppling her chair.

Jace jumped back, hands raised in front of him, eyes wide.

"Sorry. I…uh…" How could she explain the sense of panic that rushed over her at the feeling of being trapped? She couldn't. She closed her eyes and inhaled deeply, grateful for the slight chill that evening brought to the cabin.

Jace frowned. "Are you okay?"

"Yes." She nodded, the ache in her chest easing now that she had some space and the past had stopped battering her. "I'm sorry. I'm extremely claustrophobic."

"No, I'm sorry, I didn't mean to crowd you." He shoved a hand through his hair and righted the chair. "Please, sit. I promise I'll give you some breathing room."

She offered a shaky smile and returned to her seat, then took a deep breath and wiped the tears she only just realized had spilled over.

As promised, he kept his distance, leaning against the back of the couch. "Did you do what I suggested before? Try to get into the killer's head, anticipate what he might do next?"

"Not yet." She caught his gaze with hers, silently pleading for him to let her momentary anxiety go. "But if you leave me alone for a little while, I think I might know a way."

"Of course." He paused, his blue eyes intense as they studied her. A small smile shimmered in the depths of his gaze. "If you're sure you're okay."

"I am, thank you." She turned away from the sincerity in his eyes, had to if she was going to immerse herself in her killer's mind the only way she knew how.

Time to start book three.

How did he choose his victims? She grabbed a spiral notebook from the top of the stack in her drawer to make notes and pulled her computer closer. She opened a new Word document and titled it *Book Three*.

Chapter One. He stood watching her. She'd change the first line later, make it something catchier, more memorable. For now, it helped give her a visual of him, watching, stalking, needing... This was her first attempt to get inside her killer's head. The first and second books had been written entirely from the heroine's point of view.

Addison closed her eyes and envisioned the woman through the killer's eyes. Why her? What drew him? What was it about her that touched some deep part of him and made him want her? Specifically her, not any other woman. The slim build? Maybe. The big smile? Perhaps. Auburn highlights reflecting the sunlight shining on her long dark hair? Bingo.

The hair. That was it. It was definitely the long dark hair. The image of that hair fanned around the victim's head had haunted Addison's nightmares for years before she'd ever started writing.

Jace stopped at the edge of the woods behind the house after running the perimeter with Phoenix, breathing a little harder than he'd like to admit. He should have kept himself in better shape over the past years. If not for running every day with Phoenix, he wouldn't have bothered exercising at all. Actually, if not for having to care for the pup who'd shown up on his doorstep not long after Jennifer's death, Jace would probably have spiraled into an even worse depression. The need to take care of Phoenix was the only thing that had dragged him out of bed some days and given him reason to pull himself out of the dull haze brought on by the alcohol. The pup had restored some of his long-lost faith and helped him to move forward.

Phoenix nudged his leg, pulling his focus away from the memories Addison had stirred, memories better left in the past.

The sun had already begun to sink past the horizon, painting the wall of windows at the back of the house in a dazzling array of colors. Once darkness fell, he'd have a perfect view of the living room from the forest. A security nightmare.

If anyone figured out where they were, he'd have a tough time protecting her. But he would protect her, no matter what it took. As long as he could stand, he'd stand in front of her. Her strength, her courage, her desire to save whomever she could, even at her own personal expense, touched him in a way he didn't understand. But he wanted to. He wanted to learn everything he could about Addison Keller.

He shook off the thought. Even if he had forgiven her for whatever role she might have played in Maris's story, even if he had wanted to pull her into his arms and shelter her from whatever nightmares haunted her, even if he was searching for a relationship, which he most definitely was not, his only concern right now should be how to keep her safe and how to stop this killer from harming anyone else.

Only one road wound up the mountain, continuing on past her cabin and stopping in a dead end with a scenic overlook a few miles up. He'd only seen one house past hers, though a small development stood toward the beginning of the road, which meant it wouldn't take the killer too long to find them now that he had an idea what direction they'd come from. The cover of the coming darkness should keep them safe for the night, but they'd have to leave by first light, before their stalker had too much of a chance to search the area.

The sun sank farther below the trees, streaking the sky in deep shades of orange and yellow and bringing Jace a sense of unease. Connor should have been there by now.

Phoenix stiffened at his side, his posture rigid, ears erect.

Jace scanned the woods, keeping some of his attention on Phoenix, waiting for any sign of danger.

After a few seconds, Phoenix shook himself and looked at Jace, whatever had alerted him apparently forgotten. No immediate threat, then. But no Connor, either.

"Come on, boy." He jogged toward the house with Phoenix at his side.

He had to search for something to feed Phoenix, just in case Connor hadn't gotten his message or didn't show up. Besides, Addison might not have eaten anything since she'd been with her. Of course, that shouldn't matter to him. Feeding her had nothing to do with security, which was all he'd agreed to provide.

In the kitchen, he washed his hands, then searched through the cabinets. Finding a large skillet, he set it on the stove. He enjoyed cooking. It relaxed him in a way nothing else did.

Addison seemed to have equipped the kitchen surprisingly well for someone who didn't seem to have much interest in eating anything. He poured a little olive oil in the bottom of the pan to heat, then added garlic from a jar in the fridge. He'd have preferred fresh garlic, along with an onion and a few diced tomatoes, but with no fresh ingredients in the house, he'd have to make do.

He wanted to get back to Addison's book. Even though he was dissecting it while reading, searching for any clue to who the next victim might be, he was also enjoying it. Probably more than he'd like to admit. She was a strong writer. Her characters had depth and her heroine was likable but with flaws, the kind of woman you'd want to see win.

He opened the package of sausage he'd taken out of the freezer to thaw that morning. Using a small knife, he slit the sausage casings and emptied the meat into the sizzling oil and garlic. He then cleaned up and started toward the pantry to search for spices. The aroma of cooking sausage filled the kitchen, making his mouth water.

Phoenix lifted his head from where he lay by the back door, alerting Jace to Addison's presence before she spoke.

"What are you doing?"

He stopped and turned to face her. "Making dinner. Some of us have to eat, you know."

She shrugged, crossed the kitchen and set her empty water glass on the counter, then lifted a mug of tea she must have made earlier and forgotten. She kept her gaze averted. "It smells good."

"Thanks."

Something about her, a certain sense of vulnerability, maybe, touched him. Not that she was weak; inner strength radiated from her, but something…

"How did your readers take you killing off the main character's sister at the end of the book?" He hadn't reached that part yet, but he was already dreading it.

He had no doubt Addison's descriptive writing would touch the reader and make them feel as if a beloved friend had died.

Her hands shook as she lifted the tea bag out and dropped it into the garbage pail. She stuck the mug in the microwave and turned it on, then turned to face him, her smile tentative. "I'd be lying if I said I didn't get my fair share of hate mail."

"You can't be serious."

"Yup. People threatened me with everything from boycotting my books to inflicting bodily harm."

"No, not about the hate mail. I meant you can't be serious about heating that old tea in the microwave."

She stared at him a moment, then laughed a little and shook her head. "My eyes are burning. Probably partly from being on the computer, but I'm tired, too. Since we don't have coffee, I thought the tea might help."

He took her mug out of the microwave, dumped the contents and filled the kettle with water. If he had to stay awake much longer, he was going to need the caffeine. "Where are the letters?"

"What letters?"

"You said you got your fair share of hate mail. What did you do with it? Did you report it to the police?"

She held his gaze and lifted a brow but said nothing.

Oh, right. For a moment he forgot who he was talking to. "Can I ask you something?"

She shrugged, the smile dancing in the gold depths of her green eyes a quick glimpse of who she might be without the stress of a killer battering her. "Sure, but I can't promise I'll answer."

"Fair enough. Feel free to tell me it's none of my business." He was a bit sorry he'd brought it up, knowing the brief flicker of happiness would disappear in an instant. "What made you turn on Brandon? Don't get me wrong, I'm glad you told Maris what was going on, but I just wondered, after being married to him for some time, what made you speak up when you did?"

She stared at the floor and shook her head. "I didn't."

He barely heard her response. "I'm sorry?"

"I didn't tell Maris anything. I didn't know."

That actually made more sense. Addison struck him as too loyal to betray someone she cared about. Yet, her sense of responsibility wouldn't have allowed her to turn a blind eye if she knew what Brandon had been guilty of.

He grinned, propped a finger under her chin and lifted her gaze to meet his. "Don't beat yourself up. I was his partner, probably spent more time with him than you did, and I didn't know, either."

She shot him a grateful smile, and he changed the subject.

"Did you keep them? The letters from your less than adoring fans?"

"Most of it came by email."

Jace stilled.

"I put it in a folder and saved it." She shrugged. "I don't know why, but I—"

"Did any of the email addresses match?"

"What?"

"The email addresses from the hate mail. Did any of them match the email addresses the killer used?" His tone was harsher than intended. He didn't mean it to sound so blunt, but this might be their first real clue.

Her eyes widened. "I…uh… I don't know. I never thought to check."

He worked to soften some of the anger in his voice. He wasn't angry with her, but if her ex hadn't bullied her continuously, she might have been able to call the police and figure this whole thing out sooner. "Can you pull it up?"

She tucked a loose strand of hair behind her ear and nodded, lowering her gaze. Tears shimmered in her eyes.

His heart ached for her. It wasn't her fault. None of this was, despite the guilt obviously weighing her down. "Truthfully, it's probably a long shot. If the killer sent the messages from three different email addresses, chances are he wouldn't have used any of them to send hate mail. But it still has to be checked."

"Is there a way you can check it?" Her voice hitched.

"I can see if any of the email addresses match, but that's about it." He shook his head. "I'm no computer expert."

She sniffed and wiped the tears from her cheeks.

"We will find him, Addison."

She nodded, her expression still somber, and he lost the battle against reaching out to her.

He gripped her ice-cold hand in his, rubbing warmth into it. "I know you don't completely trust me, but have faith in God. We'll find the killer, and we'll stop him."

"And then what?"

"What do you mean?"

"What happens after we find him, *if* we do? Do I return to writing? Do I write another book some other killer might emulate?"

He cradled her cheek and used his thumb to wipe her tears. "I can't answer that for you, Addison. Only you can decide where to go from here, with a lot of soul-searching, I imagine. But I don't think you should let anyone take away something you obviously love, something you're quite good at."

A tentative smile softened her features.

Even though he knew what her answer would be, and reluctantly agreed with her to some extent, he had to try. "Are you sure you don't want to go to the police?"

She jerked back as if he'd slapped her.

He instantly wished he could take back the suggestion, though he knew he couldn't. "If we're going to catch this killer, we need more resources than you and I have. We also need more manpower. We're pressed for time, and we need help from somewhere."

Jace hadn't walked back into a police station since the day he'd resigned. Even then, he hadn't known whom he could trust, so he had no one to turn to now. But if they went to the police in Shady Creek, maybe that wouldn't matter. He swallowed hard, forcing the next words past the lump of resentment threatening to choke him. "I'll go with you."

"You don't understand." Tears darkened her lower lashes, shimmering in the fading light from the window.

"Then tell me. Help me understand."

"It's not that I don't want to cooperate. I desperately want this killer to be found and stopped. And I would do anything…" She held his gaze, anger burning in her eyes. "Anything at all, no matter the personal cost, to stop him. But the police won't help me. No matter which station we go into, at the end of the day, the SCPD is in charge of this investigation. The killings took place in their jurisdiction, on Brandon's turf."

She wasn't wrong about the jurisdiction, and he didn't hold a high opinion of some of his fellow officers, which was why he was no longer on the force, but he couldn't imagine them turning their backs on potential information about a killer. "No matter what happened between you and your ex, no cop is going to ignore evidence that might lead them to a serial killer."

"Brandon has a lot of pull. One of his buddies already insinuated I was behind the murders when he questioned me."

He had to concede that was true. The man had half the force in his pocket, and those he didn't control were too afraid of the consequences to cross him. Jace was living proof of the power the man held. "There's no love lost between Brandon and me, but he has nothing to do with this."

Her laughter held no humor. "You and Brandon? I thought you two were partners, though that didn't stop him from trying to take you down with him."

Anger surged through him in a wave he had no hope of controlling, and he trembled with the need to dull it. "*Instead* of him."

"What?"

"He tried to take me down instead of him, because I wouldn't indulge in the…activities he so enjoyed once I found out what was going on. Unfortunately, no one would stand against him with me, and he tried to set me up to take the fall for his illegal pursuits." He clenched his fists, willing the rage to the small compartment he'd created to contain it.

"It didn't work, because I quit. I walked away from my career, the people I thought were my friends, my self-respect…and then Jennifer was killed. A warning? Or maybe my punishment for crossing him." Maybe Brandon had been concerned Jace would keep talking if he went to jail. Maybe he was afraid the right— or wrong, in his mind—person would listen. So he'd given him a warning, because there were other people in the world Jace loved, too: Connor, Connor's parents, who'd taken him in when his world had shattered and provided a loving home.

And once he'd walked away, he'd been acquitted along with Brandon and the rest of them.

He turned away, unable to face her, unwilling to see the pity in her eyes.

"No one walks away from Brandon unscathed," she said softly.

"I know." Just because his scars didn't show didn't mean there were none. God knew he carried his share.

"You really don't get it, do you?" She wrapped her arms around herself, pain and fear evident in her stance. "There is no way Brandon will allow anyone to help me. A killer is after me. If he's not found, he'll kill me, unless I…"

She waved away whatever she'd been about to say. "Brandon would love nothing more than to see me dead, especially at the hand of a killer I created. For all I know, he hired someone to play the part. That would be just like Brandon. Let someone else do the dirty work, then walk away if he gets caught. Ideally, Brandon wins. But, trust me on this, he *never* loses."

Without waiting for her tea, Addison turned and walked away, her back rigid, stress bunching the muscles in her shoulders.

He watched her leave, then leaned his hands on the counter and lowered his head between his arms, wrestling the anger and pain under control. He had to find a way to control the rage, to let go of the past, to forgive all of those who had harmed him, especially those who had turned away out of fear for their own safety. Could he blame them, really?

The smell of sausage cooking turned his stomach. He needed to think. He stirred the fully browned meat, then rubbed a hand over his scratchy five-o'clock shadow. He needed a shave. If Connor didn't get there soon, he'd have to ask Addison to sit right outside the bathroom door, where he could hear her if she screamed, while he took a shower.

Ignoring the urge to break something, he headed to the pantry for spices. Garlic powder, sundried tomato and basil—hmm…that might work—a few cans of tomato sauce. He grabbed what he needed in both hands and turned, lifting his elbow to shut off the light.

He headed back to the kitchen with the spices and sauce and dropped them onto the counter beside the stove, then added what he needed to the sausage and stirred.

Addison wasn't the only victim Brandon had left in his wake.

But Jace had allowed Brandon to take everything from him. Maybe if he'd fought harder…

It wasn't like Connor had abandoned Jace when the scandal came to light. He'd stood by him, had offered help. Once he'd left the Marine Corps, Connor had opened his own private investigation firm, and he'd even offered Jace a job.

Jace had turned him down. He'd been so absorbed in feeling sorry for himself, he'd pushed away the one man who might have believed in him. Then Connor had buddied up with Maris, supposedly trying to prove the allegations she'd wielded against Brandon. Her story must have been very convincing, because Connor had come to Jace then, had confronted him, asked him if the charges she'd made against him were true, begged him to be honest if he'd been involved in any crimes.

Jace, his mind dulled by alcohol, his emotions raw from grief, had blown up, seeing the question as a betrayal. Looking back, he could see more clearly. Connor hadn't accused, he'd simply asked. But Jace had been too stubborn to understand the difference.

Addison's scream jolted him back to the present. Her next scream propelled him through the doorway, weapon drawn.

SEVEN

Blackness weighed heavily, pinning her down. Fear held her immobile. She clenched her teeth hard, desperate to hold back the scream.

She had to move, had to help. She had to get out of there before the darkness crushed her. She curled into a tighter ball, tears streaming down her cheeks, trying to keep her sobs soft enough so he wouldn't hear, wouldn't find her. She had to hide.

Had to help.

The smell of blood surrounded her, seeping to her along with a small sliver of light. Terrified, shaking, silent, she pressed one eye against the crack, peeked. Blood covered the floor, dark hair fanned around—

"Addison!"

She squeezed her eyes closed, blocking the image.

"Addison, come on." Strong hands gripped her arms, shook her.

No. She had to stay hidden, couldn't respond. The voice, so familiar. She wanted to reach for him, wanted to lose herself in the safety of... No! Mommy said to hide. She had to listen...had to hide...had to help.

"Addison! Wake up, now!"

The scream welled within her until her lungs would

no longer contain it, then it ripped free with such force it tore Addison from the nightmare.

Hands clutched her throat. No, not hands…hair. Her hair had wrapped around her neck while she'd slept. She jerked up on the couch, clawed at it, tried to untangle it from her throat.

"Hold on, Addison. Stop." Though Jace's command was a bit rough, his touch was gentle as he lifted her hands away, then worked to unwind her hair from where it had settled across her throat. "Take it easy, now. I have you. Everything's fine."

Addison sucked in a shaky breath. Not enough air. She needed more. Disoriented, she scanned the room. Hadn't she been working? Her desk chair had been pushed back, her laptop closed.

"Addison?"

Her gaze shot to his.

Jace smiled, but his eyes remained somber, narrowed in concern. "That must have been some dream."

His voice remained calm, steadying her as he tucked the last strands of hair behind her ear and sat back, close enough to still offer comfort, yet far enough to allow her the space she needed to breathe. "Are you all right now?"

She nodded. Heat crept up her cheeks. How could she explain the nightmares she'd suffered since childhood?

He flopped back against the couch cushion, totally at ease, and propped his feet on the large ottoman. Surely he'd be more alert, if there was any threat? "I have a little experience with nightmares, and I'm a good listener if you want to talk."

Phoenix stood nearby, hovering but not agitated.

Her first instinct was to blow Jace off. After all, everyone suffered nightmares. Jace had just admitted he did, but something about her nightmares seemed important. Addison sat up straighter and curled into the corner of the couch. Shivering, she pulled a throw around her. "My eyes started to burn, so I grabbed a notebook to work on plotting and came to sit on the couch. I must have fallen asleep."

Jace got up and searched for a second, then lifted her notebook from the floor, found her pen stuck between two cushions. He closed the book, tucked the pen into the spirals and set it aside on the ottoman before returning to his place. "It's really not surprising you'd have a nightmare after all you've been through."

"That's just it—the nightmare is nothing new. I've suffered with them for as long as I can remember."

He sat up straighter. "Are they always the same?"

She shrugged. She'd never spoken about her nightmares to anyone, not even Maris, when her sister used to lie beside her at night and stay awake as long as she could so Addison could sleep. A dull ache gripped her heart. She was going to have to make up with Maris, forgive her for doing what she must have thought was the right thing. Who knew? Maybe it was. She might have failed to take Brandon down, but at least Addison had realized what a monster he was. "The nightmares are always some variation of the same thing. I'm trapped in an enclosed space, the smell of blood surrounding me, cloying, choking me."

"Can you ever remember actually feeling trapped somewhere, even if it was only figuratively?"

Sharp pain pierced her temples. She jumped to her feet, tossing the throw aside. "I… Could you give me a few minutes to freshen up, please?"

He studied her for another moment while she silently pleaded for him to let this drop. He then stood.

"Sure thing. If you're sure you're okay, I'm going to finish dinner."

She headed to the small bathroom to splash water on her face and finger-comb her hair. Trapped. She couldn't remember ever being trapped anywhere, and yet a vague familiarity with the space she inhabited in her dream had always plagued her after waking. For a while, after her marriage had ended, she'd thought the nightmares had stopped, believed maybe it was her marriage she'd felt trapped in and Brandon was the attacker she'd sought to hide from, but then the nightmares had started again not long after she'd moved out. Question was, why? Did she still fear him, or was it something else stalking her dreams? The same thing that had stalked her nightmares since she was a child?

She returned to the kitchen a little while later, her eyes red and slightly puffy, though for the most part she'd pulled herself together. "Can I help with anything?"

"There's not much to do, but you can set the table if you want." He filled a big pot with water and put it on the stove to boil, then grabbed a box of pasta from the pantry.

"If we had supplies, I'd make salad to go with the pasta, but this will have to do for tonight." He held up a loaf of Italian bread. "I found it in the freezer."

He cut the bread in half and opened it, then left it on the butcher-block countertop while he mixed butter, garlic powder and a few other spices she couldn't see, from where she stood at the table, into a small bowl. "Do you like garlic bread?"

"Mmm-hmm." She set a couple of plates on the breakfast bar and added napkins and silverware.

The aroma of sauce cooking filled the kitchen. She

sat on a stool and watched him. His movements were practiced and comfortable. Cooking obviously wasn't new to him. She'd never had a man working in her kitchen before. It was…interesting.

Brandon didn't cook, nor did he do dishes. Those were a woman's responsibilities, along with cleaning, laundry, entertaining his company… Brandon could have afforded an army of housekeepers—which she probably should have questioned, since his salary shouldn't have been enough to give him the lifestyle he enjoyed—but he'd lectured her often about earning her keep, even though he wouldn't allow her to work.

She shifted on the stool, uncomfortable with the thought of someone else allowing her to do something. He hadn't actually said she couldn't work; he'd just made life miserable for her and everyone around her if she tried, making it impossible for her to keep a job. She didn't mind doing the housework. It was better than sitting alone hour after hour, day after day. Besides, a housekeeper would have been a witness to the realities of her marriage, an intrusion on the fantasy Addison had chosen to embrace.

The one thing she hadn't allowed him to take away from her, the one thing she'd stood strong about, was going to church. Each week she went to mass and prayed for him, prayed for guidance, and when the time came, she'd prayed she'd have the strength to do what needed to be done and the courage to stand up to him.

She pushed the thoughts aside. None of it mattered now. Had she known what he was when she married him, she wouldn't have. If she'd realized what a monster he was sooner, she would have left. Immersed in the situation, she hadn't been able to see the truth; she'd simply accepted the way things were and excused his behavior, choosing to live in blissful ignorance rather than fight a losing battle. She pressed a hand to her lower back, the phantom pain a subtle but constant reminder of what happened when you engaged in any kind of confrontation with Brandon. Denial had been her most consistent companion throughout her marriage.

"Did you hear me?"

She jumped, startled from the past, Jace's deep voice bringing momentary panic. "I'm sorry."

He frowned at her.

She forced a smile, grimace, whatever. "I wasn't paying attention."

"We're going to have to figure out what to do. If you don't go talk to the police—"

She shot to her feet. "I already told y—"

"I know." He held up his hands, butter knife gripped in one, in a gesture of surrender. "I'm not saying you should, I'm just saying we have to figure out what we're going to do if you don't."

She lifted a brow and kept her expression serious, suppressing the genuine smile tugging at her. "We?"

He grinned. "Whatever."

Jace obviously planned on sticking around. She ignored the flutter that brought. Her laughter escaped, despite the fear that had been consuming her only moments before. Something about Jace made her want to trust him, a dangerous proposition considering the situation.

Phoenix jumped to his feet, hackles raised, a low growl rumbling in his chest.

Jace turned off the stove and slid the saucepan off the burner. Eyeing the big dog with its teeth bared, he hit the button to turn off the oven. "Get down."

Addison crouched behind the breakfast bar, keeping

the center island between her and the windows above the sink and in the back door.

"What is it?" she whispered, straining to hear over the dog's growls and the pounding of her own heart.

Jace rounded the counter, gun drawn, expression hard, the seemingly good-natured man who'd been making dinner in her kitchen only moments ago a distant memory. The drastic change was a stark reminder people weren't always what they seemed.

Brandon could speak with eloquence and sincerity that would win over the most jaded adversary. She'd lost track of the number of women who'd commented on how fortunate she was to have such a charming husband. To be fair, she couldn't argue the fact. He was charming. Too bad it was all an act.

Phoenix charged from the kitchen, his deep bark resonating off the high ceilings in the living room.

"Stay there." Jace gestured for Addison to wait and followed the big dog.

Yeah, right. She grabbed a butcher knife from the block on the counter. Keeping her head low, she scrambled across the kitchen and lunged through the archway after him.

The back window exploded inward, sending shards of glass flying everywhere.

"Get down!" Jace dove toward Addison, caught her around the waist and shoved her to the floor beneath him. He had to get her to safety before he could go after whomever was out there. He half pushed, half dragged her behind the couch, then jumped up and pulled his gun. "Stay down."

Jace bolted for the back of the house, crouching low, careful to stay clear of the line of windows.

"What happened?" Addison kept her head low.

"Something came through the window." He had to get her somewhere safer and go after this guy.

"Do you know what it was?"

Jace shook his head. "Couldn't tell. It sounded big, though, so not a bullet."

Keeping to the side, Jace ripped the back door open. A light bobbed through the woods in the distance, accompanied by the sounds of retreat. "Addison, take Phoenix with you, get in the bathroom and lock the door."

She obeyed instantly, keeping her head beneath the level of the couch as she scrambled to do as he'd instructed.

"Don't open that door for anyone but me." The instant he heard the lock click, he bolted for the back door. Even though she'd taken the big knife with her, he hated the idea of leaving her and Phoenix alone and unprotected, but he had no choice. He locked the door behind him and ran across the dark yard, keeping to the shadows as much as possible, but not being as careful as he should have been.

"Sounds like a bear crashing through the woods," he muttered to himself as he ran, glancing over his shoulder in case a second threat loomed behind him and trying to keep an eye on the house in case another suspect lurked in the darkness. Though it seemed the killer had acted alone so far—things would have played out a lot differently if he'd had a partner when he'd come after them the last time—Jace couldn't rule it out. And he'd left Addison at the house.

He had no choice, had to go after the killer, and yet… It didn't make sense. Something was wrong.

Jace ran along the grass on the border of the yard,

parallel to the line the suspect was following, easily keeping track of the flashlight's beam. While the suspect tripped over brush and got snagged by branches, Jace had no trouble catching up.

Muffled curses reached him as he silently stalked the man. Something was definitely wrong. No way this bumbling fool planned and executed two murders, then managed to elude the police. Doubt crept in. Unless Addison was right. Maybe the cops weren't investigating it properly. But why? Could Brandon be behind it? Brandon was a lot of things, but he wasn't a fool.

The suspect stumbled out onto the road just past the end of the driveway. Not wanting to be blinded by the flashlight beam when the suspect turned, Jace slid behind a huge tree trunk bordering the driveway, gun ready. He chanced a quick glance over his shoulder. He'd locked the door on his way out, and the hole in the back window wasn't big enough for a man to get through. He hadn't heard the sounds of anyone breaking in or Addison screaming, though he could still hear Phoenix's muffled barking. Satisfied she was okay for the moment, Jace turned his full attention to the man standing on the side of the road.

After quickly scanning the area, the suspect turned the flashlight off and stuffed it into his jacket pocket, then strolled along the road heading down the mountain.

You have got to be kidding me. Enough of this. Jace stepped from behind the tree, holding the gun ready in a two-handed stance. "Freeze."

The guy stopped.

"Hands out to the side where I can see them and turn around. Slowly."

He did exactly as Jace instructed. When he spotted the gun, the guy shot his hands into the air and started backing up. "No, man. It's not what you think. It wasn't me. Well, it was, but not what you think. Don't shoot me, man."

"Don't move." Jace crept toward him.

"No, no. Okay. I'll stay still." Tremors shook the man's…no, not a man—the kid's voice. He stopped backpedaling. "Just don't shoot."

Jace approached him, still staying a safe distance back, and lowered his weapon. "Start talking."

The boy, who couldn't be more than fifteen, rubbed a shaking hand over his head, pulling his sweatshirt hood off. He spun around and ran. Fast.

"Great." Shoving the gun in his waistband, Jace took off after him.

The kid stayed on the road, the downhill slope adding to his momentum, and he started to pull away from Jace.

Jace ran faster. No way was this kid getting away. He might be their only lead, might be the only way to stop this killer. Might be the only way to keep Addison safe. And yet Jace couldn't chase him much longer; he had to get back to the house in case the killer had used the kid to lure him out.

Headlights washed over the scene from behind him, and Jace moved onto the shoulder without slowing, ready to dive for cover.

The car passed Jace, swung around the kid and fishtailed, its back end swinging out as it skidded to a stop in front of him.

Unable to slow his stride, the kid plowed into the side of the car, bounced off and landed flat on his back in the middle of the street.

The driver's door swung open and Connor jumped out. He grinned at Jace. "Getting slow in your old age, huh?"

Jace stopped and bent at the waist, hands on his knees, sucking in huge gulps of air. As soon as he could breathe again, he'd straighten Connor out.

Connor reached out a hand and helped the kid to his feet, then shoved his back against the car, keeping a hand splayed against the kid's chest. "Do not run again."

The kid only nodded, chest heaving, bringing Jace a small rush of relief. Maybe he wasn't in as bad a shape as he thought. *Yeah, right.*

He rubbed a hand over his mouth and approached the kid. "Talk. Now."

The kid's head nodded frantically, like a bobblehead. "It wasn't me. Some old dude paid me to throw it."

"Throw what?"

"The rock, man. He gave me fifty bucks and said if I came up here tonight and threw that rock through the big window when a woman was in the living room, he'd give me another fifty."

Addison! "When?"

The kid shrugged and swiped the hair that had fallen into his eyes. "I don't know, 'round dinnertime, I guess. Five, maybe six."

He had to get back to her. Also had to have answers. "Get in the car."

Connor ripped the back door open.

"Don't hurt me, man, I needed the money, ya know."

"Now."

The kid dove into the car and slid across the back seat. Jace jumped in after him.

Connor slammed the door, rounded the car and jumped into his own seat.

"Go, go, go!" They had to get to Addison. The killer could be there already.

"What's wrong?" Maris spun around in the passenger seat and pinned him with a glare.

Ignoring her, he turned to the kid. "Are you supposed to meet him somewhere?"

"Nah, man…" Knowledge started to dawn in the kid's expression. "Well, hey, fifty bucks is fifty bucks, and all I had to do was come up here and throw a rock through a window."

Jace reined in his temper. It wouldn't help anything, and it wasn't the kid's fault he'd been played. Though it was certainly his fault he'd agreed to damage Addison's property, he hadn't been trying to hurt her. "What'd the guy look like?"

"I don't know."

Jace gripped the front of the boy's shirt. He needed answers.

The kid held his hands up. "Honest, mister. I don't know. He was taller than me and kinda big, but that's all I can tell you. He had on a long black coat, sunglasses and a really bad wig. Oh, and a big fake mustache and beard." The kid grinned. "Ain't no one could grow a mustache and beard like that, dude."

Jace let go of the kid. Now what? He couldn't just release him. What if the killer came after him? Yet he couldn't detain him, either.

Relief rushed through him as Connor rocketed up the driveway toward the house. Except for the kid's soft sobs as he must have realized how much trouble he might be in, everything seemed quiet.

"I'm going to pull right up—"

The world exploded, towers of flame shooting up across the front lawn, blocking his view of the house. Heat assailed him as he dove from the car and ran toward the inferno. "Addison!"

EIGHT

Phoenix barked frantically, pausing only long enough to growl as he stood guard at the closed bathroom door. He turned back to Addison, looked up at her as if to ask why she was just standing there doing nothing, and returned to barking.

"Good question, boy." But what could she do? Jace had said to stay put, and he was probably right. Though he'd left Phoenix to protect her, what could the dog do against a gun? No way could she live with herself if she got him hurt…or worse.

"It's okay, boy," she soothed, as much for her own sake as his. She ran a hand along his flank. "We'll just wait here for Jace to get back."

What was taking so long? What if the killer got him? Her heart stuttered at the thought. She shoved it away.

Even with the light on, the walls in the small powder room closed in on her. Sweat dripped down the sides of her face. She gripped the knife tighter in both hands, clutching it to her chest. Could she use it? If a killer ripped the door open right now, could she use the knife to end his life? *Thou shalt not kill.* Or would she die hugging it against her, useless?

The dog's agitation generated a heat of its own as he paced back and forth in front of the door.

Addison shoved her hair back with her wrist, unwilling to release her hold on the weapon for even an instant. She pressed her back against the wall.

Phoenix jumped against the door, clawing the wood, over and over.

"Phoenix, no." She gripped his collar, tried to turn his face toward her in an attempt to ease his distress.

Her sweat-soaked shirt clung to her. Why was she so hot? Anxiety?

Phoenix clawed wildly, barking, barking…

"Phoenix, please, boy, what's wrong?" She couldn't think. Had to think.

Think, think, think…

Darkness pressed in on her. A sliver of light peeked through a small crack. No, not real. Blackness weighed heavily, threatening to suffocate her. The bathroom light was on. Not real. Nightmare and reality swirled together in a dizzying array, tugging her in different directions. Hide. Help. Run. Hide. Jace said to hide. Mommy said to hide. Had to help. Jace might be in trouble.

A puddle of blood. Dark hair splayed through it. A face turned away. Familiar. Jace? No! M—

Phoenix gripped her arm in his mouth, startling her from whatever nightmare held her immobile, and pulled her toward the door.

The smell of smoke assailed her. Her breath whooshed out, sucking all the air from her lungs. Fire. That was what she'd missed, unable to think past the claustrophobia.

Phoenix released her and barked.

"Okay, boy." She patted his head. "I'm okay now."

He whimpered and returned to pacing in front of the door.

She pressed a hand against it. Cool. The flames hadn't reached her yet.

All right. Think. Where in the game were they? This was too early. That was why she'd missed it. After the third murder, the killer had tried to burn her house down. He'd ringed the lawn around the house with accelerant and ignited it, the flames taunting her as they moved closer and closer, surrounding her. Stalking her.

Had the killer escalated? Had he already killed the third woman? No. It was too soon.

She had to pull herself together, had to think. If he'd escalated, she was too late to save the third victim. She sobbed and slammed her entwined fists against the door. "No!"

Light flashed from the knife's blade. The killer didn't have a death wish, so he'd have set the fire and remained outside the circle. He might be sitting in a tree waiting to shoot her if she emerged, but a knife wouldn't help with that, and he wouldn't be in the house.

She set the knife on the counter and gripped Phoenix's collar. She didn't have his leash, and she couldn't risk him running off and getting hurt. "You have to stay by my side. Understand?"

The big dog steadied and pressed against her leg.

"Please, God, help me find a way to save him," she whispered as she cracked the door open a fraction of an inch. "And please let Jace be okay."

He should have returned by now. But even if he had, he wouldn't be able to get to her if the killer had mimicked the scene in her book. The entire house would be surrounded by a circle of fire. If Jace had been inside the ring, he'd already have reached her. The killer had lured him out so he could get to her.

Though the flames hadn't yet reached the house, smoke poured in through the gaping hole in the back window. Since Phoenix stayed glued to her side, she released his collar and searched the area for whatever the killer had thrown through the window.

A dark green stone sat amid the shattered glass. Careful to avoid getting cut, she used a throw from the couch to pick it up and wrap it. Maybe Jace would be able to get fingerprints, though what they'd do with them, she had no idea. Maybe an anonymous letter to the police.

If, of course, she could find a way out of there.

Smoke stung the back of her throat, and she coughed. Tears streamed down her face, and she squinted against the burning in her eyes.

She gathered the last few throws from the couch, hurried to the kitchen and dumped them in the sink. Keeping low, out of view of the window just in case, she ran the water and soaked the throws. "I'm going to put this over you, okay, Phoenix?"

The dog looked up into her eyes and whined.

She kissed his head and tossed the soaking wet throw over him. "It's okay, boy, I'll get you out of this."

She threw a second wet throw over her head and shoulders, carrying the last one and the wrapped stone with her as they headed through the kitchen. Even though she didn't think the killer would be able to see her through the smoke and flames, she crouched behind the couch as she made her way through the living room. The wall of windows raised the hairs on the back of her neck. She should have brought the knife. Too late.

She cracked the front door open. Flames roared into

the sky, only yards from the front porch. "Phoenix, stay."

He whimpered but obeyed.

"Addison!" Jace's screams drowned out the roar of the flames. He was okay.

Oh, God, thank You!

"I'm here, Jace." Leaving the stone and the extra throw in the doorway with Phoenix, she hurried down the length of the porch, keeping close to the house and holding a corner of the wet throw against her mouth and nose. She ran down the porch steps, missed the bottom one and twisted her ankle.

Ignore the pain. There's no time.

She grabbed the hose, unwound it from the holder as fast as she could and turned it on. Water sputtered, then poured from the hose in a steady stream. She said a silent thank-you as she ran toward the flames. All they needed was a small gap, if she could just hold the flames back long enough for them to slip through. "Are you there, Jace?"

"Addison?"

"Over here." She left the hose on the ground and ran back to the doorway for the rock. "Phoenix, come."

He trotted to her side.

She ran back, grabbed the hose and sprayed a steady stream of water at the base of an area of flames, soaking the ground as much as possible. As soon as she saw the smallest gap, she urged Phoenix through. Battling the encroaching flames, she wrapped the wet throw she was wearing tight around her, clutched the stone and dove through the flames.

Jace tackled her to the ground the instant she emerged, rolling her and ripping the throw from around her. He staggered to his feet and stamped out the small flare of flames closest to her. "Are you all right? Are you hurt?"

He patted her down, making sure there were no embers left to ignite, feeling for himself that she was whole and unharmed, then reached out a hand.

Her hand shook as she reached for him, let him help her to her feet. "I'm okay, Jace. Phoenix?"

"He's fine." He gestured toward the car parked across the lawn, where Connor held the door for Phoenix to scramble into the back seat. "Thank you."

She captured his gaze with hers, held him enraptured. "I'm sorry."

"Sorry? For what?" A black line of soot or dirt spotted her cheek. He wiped it away, his fingers lingering as he pressed his forehead against hers. They had to go, had to run. Even with Connor having their backs, they were targets out there in the open, but he couldn't turn away from her.

"I'm sorry I brought all of this on you."

"Addison…"

She squeezed her eyes closed and a soft sob escaped.

"Addison, look at me." He cradled her face between his hands, tilted it up toward him and stared into her eyes. The fear shining in hers begged him to retreat, to take her somewhere safe, to… "This is not your fault. None of it. Do you understand me? I'm here because I choose to be here, to help. Before I… Well, before I resigned, I dedicated my life to protecting others. This is no different."

Except it was. His emotions then didn't even touch the jumble of feelings that had torn through him when he'd realized he couldn't get to her and might not be able to reach her in time. A shiver tore through him. "Come on, now. We have to go."

As they fled toward the car, the feeling of a giant bull's-eye on his back was the easiest for him to deal with. At least that he understood.

Jace held the car door open for Addison to get into the back seat, then slid in behind her and closed the door.

Connor barreled down the driveway, keeping a close eye on his rearview mirror. "Is anyone hurt?"

"I'm okay." Addison buried her head in the thick fur around Phoenix's neck.

"We're fine." Jace reached his arm around her to pet Phoenix. He'd checked the dog after he'd bounded through the wall of flames, but Jace needed the reassurance.

"So…" Maris twisted around in the passenger seat to face them. "Now what?"

Jace dropped his head back and closed his eyes.

Addison stayed where she was.

Sirens blared in the distance. Connor must have called the fire department.

"All righty, then." The sound of Maris turning back around and flopping against the seat was followed by deafening silence.

Jace tried to process everything that had happened. He bolted upright, and his eyes shot open. "Hey. What happened to the kid?"

"He took off…" Connor's gaze met his in the rearview mirror. "I'm not sure when. Maris and I jumped out of the car right behind you, and he was gone when we got back to it with Phoenix."

Jace massaged the bridge of his nose. Okay, then,

nothing they could do about that. "Where are we going?"

"A motel not far from here, maybe half an hour. Private enough." And with that, conversation ceased until they pulled up to a two-story cottage surrounded by gardens and woods.

"I'll go get the keys." Maris climbed out of the car and slammed the door behind her with a little more force than necessary.

Addison jumped. "Do you mind if I take Phoenix for a walk?"

"Are you sure you're okay?" She hadn't uttered a word since they'd gotten into the car.

She nodded, her lips pressed into a firm line. "I just need some air."

Something in the plea assured him she wanted to get that air alone. He looked around the quiet grounds, then got out and held the door for her. "Go ahead, but don't go far, okay? If you stay right in the courtyard, where it's well lit, I'll be able to see you the whole time."

She nodded again, tucked her hair behind her ear and started off with Phoenix at her side.

"Just tell him, 'Heel,' and he'll fall into step beside you," he called.

She waved over her shoulder and issued the command.

Connor started past him in the direction Maris had gone, but Jace stopped him with a hand against his chest. "I want answers, Connor. Now."

Connor gestured toward the door. Dark circles ringed his bloodshot eyes. "Can we at least go inside where there's a chance we won't be gunned down before I finish explaining?"

Jace watched Addison walk the perimeter of the courtyard. "You weren't followed."

"No, but the car was left unattended for a brief span of time while we tried to find a way through the flames."

"Maybe the killer planted a bug in the car after he torched the house."

Connor seemed to contemplate that for a moment. "It's possible."

"Addison!" He waved her over, keeping a close eye on the surrounding woods.

Maris returned with three keys and handed them to Connor. "We're on the second floor, the last three rooms on the end."

Addison hurried toward him, and he kicked himself for the wide-eyed look of fear she wore. "Is something wrong?"

"No. We just want to get you inside. Just to be safe." He led her toward the rooms Maris had indicated.

An outdoor stairway led to the second-floor porch, which crossed the front of the building and wrapped around both sides. Not great from a security standpoint. Easy enough for a sniper to sit in a tree and wait them out, then take his shot as soon as they stepped outside.

But they had to have a few hours to rest, to talk, to make a plan for what would come next.

As soon as he settled Addison in the middle room, he'd ditch Connor's car at the closest hotel. Connor could probably have someone drop off another before they were ready to take off in the morning.

He opened the door to Addison's room. Clean enough, with a queen-size bed and a couch. A small table with four chairs sat in front of the window. He dragged the curtains across what was sure to be a beautiful view come morning and gestured toward the chairs. "All right, we're inside. Talk."

Connor held up his hands up in a gesture of surrender. "I'll tell you everything I know."

Jace tossed the keys onto the table and folded his arms across his chest.

"I'm going to take a shower." Addison headed for the bathroom.

"I guess that's my cue." Maris twirled her key around her finger. "Nice to see you, too, Jace."

Connor walked her next door, let her into their room, and returned to Jace. He propped his hands on his hips, his stance stiffening. "What happened to you, Jace?"

"Me? What are you talking about? I haven't heard from you in more than four years…" Caught off guard by the accusation in his tone, Jace bristled. He lifted a finger and took a step closer. "Then, out of nowhere, you call and beg me to go babysit a woman I figured probably had a large hand in destroying my life. That's some nerve you've got there, buddy."

Connor laughed and scrubbed a hand over his near crew cut. "I'm not in the mood for this, Jace, so back off." He slapped away the finger Jace still held an inch from his face and stared hard into his eyes, jaw clenched.

With his anger fueled by Connor's laughter, Jace tensed, long past ready for this fight.

Then Connor's demeanor changed. His posture, usually rigid, slumped, and he blew out a breath. "Look, man, I understand you're angry, but you walked away without giving me a chance to explain. You wouldn't take my calls, wouldn't answer your door, wouldn't listen to anything I had to say. What did you want me to do?"

"There was nothing to explain."

"Yeah, Jace, there was." He shook his head and finally broke eye contact, lowering his gaze to the floor and pressing his thumb and forefinger to his eyes. "I'm sorry. I should have tried harder to get in touch with you. I was so angry…and hurt that you wouldn't listen to me. You were the closest thing I ever had to a brother, and I felt like you betrayed me."

"*I* betrayed *you*?"

Connor squirmed. "Okay, I can understand how you might not see it that way, but maybe if you'd given me a chance to explain…"

Jace threw up his hands and turned away, needing a minute to collect himself before this mess escalated any further. The sound of running water and knocking pipes assured him Addison was safe. Although, why that mattered so much, he had no clue. Jace was free. It didn't really matter what Connor had to say. He'd done what he promised and kept Addison safe until he could pawn her off on Connor. She was no longer his problem. So why couldn't he walk away? He should be able to, and yet… He turned back to find Connor studying him. "You know what? It doesn't matter. I'm going to take a shower, and then I'm outta here."

He started past Connor toward the door, praying he would fall for Jace's bluff. There was no way he would abandon Addison with a killer on the loose, but he needed some space, at least for a few minutes.

"Wait." Connor grabbed his arm and spun him around.

Jace lowered his gaze to the hand on his arm, then lifted it back to Connor.

"I need help."

The underlying plea in the admission held his temper in check. Barely. "Then talk. Fast."

No matter what had driven a wedge between them, Jace would no more leave his brother in danger than he would Addison. Or Maris. Or anyone else.

"I think Maris is being targeted by a serial killer."

"Yeah, I already figured that out. Now tell me something I don't know."

Connor's eyes widened in surprise, then lit up with his grin. "I figured you would, though I have to admit I thought it'd take a little longer."

Some of the tension seeped from Jace. "You always did underestimate me."

"Yeah, well… Look, Jace, I meant what I said. I'm sorry. I should have tried harder to get in touch with you. I owed you an explanation for why I started working with Maris." His Adam's apple bobbed with the effort to swallow, and he shrugged. "I let my pride get in the way, and for that, I really am sorry."

Jace couldn't sustain the level of anger that self-pity had allowed him over the past years. "Whatever, Connor."

"No, not whatever. Believe me, when I met Maris, I harbored just as much anger toward her as you did, but then I gave her a chance to explain. It wasn't what you thought, Jace. She was trying to protect her sister. How could I hold that against her?"

Jace fidgeted, uncomfortable with Connor's sincerity, with the vulnerability in his expression. "And you couldn't just forgive her and move on? You had to marry her, man?"

Connor laughed. "You obviously don't know Maris Halloway."

Jace's tension ratcheted down another notch.

Then Connor sobered. "There was an incident, and Addison was hurt. I don't know all of the details. Even

Maris didn't know for sure, but it scared her. Addison was too trusting, believed everything Brandon said. Maris was terrified there would come a time Addison would stumble on proof of what a monster he was and confront him over it rather than seek help. She was too vulnerable, Jace, and Maris was afraid he would end up killing her. Can you try to understand that? If you thought someone was going to kill me, you'd have done the same thing, no matter who else was hurt in the process."

He couldn't argue with that. If someone had been a threat to Connor, Jace would have used whatever means necessary to remove the threat, no matter what.

"I need help, Jace, and I don't know anyone else I can trust as much as I do you." Connor shrugged and held his gaze. "You've always been there when I needed you, were there when I asked for help even after we haven't spoken in years. There's absolutely no doubt in my mind you'd always have my back."

A sense of betrayal still smoldered beneath the surface, but Jace tamped it down before it could flare again. "What do you need?"

"You'll help?"

"I didn't say that. It depends on what you need."

Connor nodded. "Fair enough."

"Now, while you figure out exactly what you need from me, I'm going to my room to take a shower. I haven't slept in two days, and I couldn't leave your problem alone long enough to shower."

"I'm surprised you didn't just handcuff her to something."

Jace laughed. No one knew him better than Connor. Usually because he'd handle the situation exactly the same way. "I didn't think I'd get away with it a second time."

Connor's laughter followed him toward the door.

Jace paused with his hand on the knob. "Oh, and don't forget to ditch the car—"

"It's already taken care of. I have one of my employees on the way to switch it with another."

Jace nodded. "Phoenix, come."

"I can't believe how big Phoenix has gotten."

Everything in Jace went still. He and Connor hadn't spoken since before he'd gotten Phoenix. "What are you talking about?"

"Uh…" Connor shot him a sheepish smile. "All right, okay, don't be angry."

Jace remained silent. Had Connor kept tabs on him all these years?

"When you wouldn't take my calls or talk to me, I got worried. I was just finishing up a case sort of near your place and decided to swing by and try again. I had the pup with me. He'd been abused and neglected by the man I took down, who was going to jail for a very long time. I was going to take him home, but when I saw you through the window, passed out on the couch, I decided it wasn't the best time to try to talk. The puppy curled up in front of the door." Connor paused and studied him. "I don't know why, but you seemed so alone, and I thought having someone to take care of might help. I waited down the road to make sure the puppy was okay until you took him in."

Jace swallowed hard past the lump clogging his throat.

Connor dropped onto one of the chairs and lowered his head. "I'm sorry, Jace. I know I could have handled things better, but I didn't know what to do."

"I'm sorry, too. I was so angry and bitter with everyone involved, that I just…" How could he explain the pain that had consumed him after Jennifer was killed? Brandon had been his friend, his partner. He'd trusted the man. And truth be told, Jace should have realized something wasn't right. If he hadn't trusted him so completely, he would have.

Then, when Connor had gotten involved with Maris while Jace was still under investigation… If he was going to be honest with himself, Maris had found the courage to do what Jace should have been able to do. "I'm sorry, Connor. You are my best friend, my brother, and I don't know what to say."

But he did know, even if it wasn't easy to force the words out. "Brandon framed me. I trusted him, and he betrayed me. Then, when Jennifer was killed—"

"I'm so sorry about Jennifer, Jace." Connor stood and laid a hand on his shoulder. "I've tried for the past four years to find her killer, spoken to the Internal Affairs investigators, done everything I could."

"But the trail went cold." Jace nodded. He already knew that, but learning Connor had been trying, too, help eased some of the animosity. "I didn't know who I could trust anymore, and I was afraid to let anyone in, afraid that if I did trust anyone, they'd meet the same fate Jennifer did."

Tears spilled down Connor's cheeks, but he made no move to wipe them away.

"I'm sorry, Connor. There is no excuse. I was a mess, and I drowned myself in the bottom of a bottle rather than finding the strength to do the right thing."

"Let's just forget it and move on." Connor clapped him on the back. "By the way, you looking for a job?"

Jace laughed and shook his head.

That had always been Connor's way. He never had a need to rehash the past, was always ready to forgive and move on. A good man who always sought to serve God and do His work. As he obviously had when he'd left Phoenix with Jace.

"Thanks, Connor. For everything, especially Phoenix." The big dog had probably been the only thing that had saved him from himself.

"No problem. That's what brothers are for. Now, about that job…"

"What kind of job?"

"Private investigator. This can be your first case."

"My only case." Because if Brandon Carlisle had any part in what was happening to Addison, Jace was going to find out about it, and this time, he'd stop Brandon. And once the SCPD was rid of the corruption rotting it from the inside, Jace would return to doing what he loved most.

Connor grinned and punched him in the arm. "I knew you'd do it."

"Yeah, well, it might give me the opportunity to take down Brandon Carlisle and return to the force." Something he should have done a long time ago. "I don't have a license, though."

"That's perfect. Just what I'm looking for right now. Someone invisible."

NINE

Addison emerged from the bathroom after her shower and glanced at the stone she'd taken from the house, still wrapped in the throw and stinking like smoke.

Maris glanced up from the edge of the bed, where she sat flipping through channels on the small TV.

"Where are Jace and Connor?"

"Jace went to shower, and Connor is right out front, making a phone call. I'm pretty sure we're leaving as soon as they get done. They don't want to hang around any longer than necessary." She returned to channel surfing.

Not knowing what else to say, Addison perched on the edge of a chair by the table, wishing she could open the curtains so she wouldn't feel so closed in. She unwrapped the stone the killer had thrown through the window and turned it over and over, careful to keep the blanket between it and her fingers, even though the chances the killer had left his fingerprints were slim to none. He hadn't in her book. Then again, he'd strayed from the time line by starting the fire early...unless he'd already killed the third victim.

It was not simply a stone but a piece of a whole image, about a foot long, textured on the top and smooth on the bottom. She lowered her head, pressed the cool, dark green rock to her forehead with both hands and squeezed her eyes closed, dread creeping up her spine.

"Are you all right?"

She gasped, startled by Maris at her side. She was far from all right. "Yeah."

Phoenix paced back and forth from one end of the room to the other, stopping occasionally, his ears twitching. He tilted his head for a moment, then continued pacing. This time, he stood alert, staring toward the door. He barked once.

The sound of Jace's voice as he called out before using the key to open the door brought a rush of relief she tried to ignore.

"Guess they're done." Maris hurried toward the door and threw her arms around Connor the instant he walked in.

She should have stopped to think what Maris might be going through, her husband out there searching for a killer Addison had unleashed. Had she really become that self-centered that she'd never even considered her sister's fear? When had she stopped putting others ahead of herself? All those years spent alone, before and after her divorce, had apparently taken their toll.

"Hey, there, boy." Jace squatted to pet Phoenix. "Did the shower help?"

Startled, Addison jumped. "What?"

"The shower?" Jace frowned. "Do you feel better now?"

"Oh, sorry. I guess I wasn't paying attention." She'd been busy watching him with Phoenix when she should have been trying to work out why the killer had deviated from the time line she'd laid out in her novel. "Yes, I feel better, thank you."

"What's that?" He pointed toward the piece in her hand as he stood and moved to stand beside her, careful to maintain enough distance to keep her from feeling trapped between him and the curtained windows.

"The thing he threw through the window." Addison placed the still-wrapped stone in his hands but didn't release her grip.

"Actually, he paid a kid fifty dollars to throw it through the window."

"Hmm…" She captured his gaze with hers. "Was the car bugged?"

"Not that we could find, but one of Connor's guys switched cars with us and we're going to move anyway."

She nodded and released the stone and his gaze.

He turned it over and studied the smooth, flat bottom. His brow furrowed. "What is this thing?"

"If my guess is correct, it's from his next victim's garden, except it isn't right."

"What do you mean?" Jace asked.

She shook her head, unable to get her thoughts straight. "He shouldn't have killed her yet. I'm not supposed to get the clues until after…"

"What's going on?" Maris came up behind her, Connor glued to her side.

"I don't know." Jace squeezed closer to Addison to allow them room until all three of them leaned over her at the small table.

A vise squeezed her chest. She spun the chair around to face them, and they finally backed up. She sucked in a deep, greedy breath.

Jace studied her for a moment and started to lift his hand, then lowered his gaze and let his hand drop to his side.

Disappointment surged. For an instant, she'd thought

he might reach out to comfort her. The thought of losing herself in Jace's strong embrace, even if only for a moment or two, appealed more than she cared to admit.

He frowned at the green rock. "So, what is this thing, and why does it have you so upset?"

"I think that's part of an alligator garden decoration. The whole alligator is actually three pieces, three separate stones—the tail, the back and the head. When you line them up in the garden, it looks like he's partially submerged. The piece you're holding—" she gestured toward the object Jace still held "—is the back. In the book, though, the killer sends the detective a picture of it as a clue after the third murder. At least, I think it's the third murder."

You'd think that with all the time she'd spent writing and editing that book, she'd remember the order of the murders, but she couldn't be positive. It had changed too many times to keep track.

"Yeah, it was the third murder. I didn't put it together, because in the book he only sent the picture." Jace set the piece on the table. "I don't remember a scene where he threw anything through the window, but I didn't finish reading yet. Did he deviate from the book again?"

"Sort of." But it didn't make sense, because the real killer couldn't know that… "The killer did pay someone fifty bucks to throw a rock—just a regular rock—through the detective's window."

Jace's gaze shot to Connor. "No wonder the little punk kept repeating that phrase about the fifty dollars. The killer told him to say it."

Addison squeezed her temples between her thumb and fingers. "Yeah, well, there's another problem."

"What's that?"

"It didn't happen until book two."

"I thought you said book two hasn't come out yet."

She held his gaze. "It hasn't."

"That changes everything." Jace grabbed a pen and pad from the nightstand and started scribbling notes on a clean page. "Who would have read the second book?"

"A lot of people. My editor, my publicist, my agent, the team who acquired it, reviewers and anyone else who received an ARC, too many—"

"Wait." Jace held up a hand. "What's an ARC?"

"An advance reader copy. Sometimes reviewers and bloggers get copies of the book ahead of time so they can read it and post reviews when it releases. Other authors also receive a copy so they can read it and offer advance praise for the book."

Seeming deflated, Jace tossed the pen and pad back onto the nightstand. "Still, it's a lot fewer people than have read the first one. Is there a list?"

Addison shrugged. "I suppose someone could figure out who it was sent to, but what about people they might have lent it to?"

"They're allowed to do that?"

"Not really, but some do. My point is, if someone really wanted a copy, they might be able to get it."

"Well, it still narrows the field."

"Plus, if the killer was the man who broke into my house, I saw him through the window, leaning over the bed where my laptop was. My files are password protected, but if he knew what he was doing, he might have been able to get a copy from there."

Silence descended on the room, each of them lost in their own thoughts. They could possibly narrow down who had read the second book. Just because she didn't give these things much thought didn't mean someone else didn't. Probably Ron or her publicist, Jerry, would know how to find out.

"Maybe we can use the stone to find the victim before he gets to her," Connor said.

Maris shook her head and frowned. "Why would he do that? Why give the clue if you can use it to locate the victim before he can kill her?"

Jace shrugged. "Maybe to up the tension."

"Or maybe because she ran." Connor took the stone from the table and examined it. "Maybe when Addison left instead of hanging around and playing his game, he decided to up the stakes, give her a clue early."

"Hmm…could be." Shoving a hand through his shaggy hair, Jace stared at the stone as if it would suddenly reveal the killer. "Maybe he's hoping to engage her by letting her think she might be able to save the next victim."

"I don't see how it will help." Addison racked her brain for any way to use the knowledge to her advantage.

"Either way, we have to figure out where the stone came from." Jace flipped through his notes.

"It's not possible." The stone had no tag offering a way to tell where it had been bought. "I saw them in a garden shop once, tons of them, then looked them up online when I was writing the story. Everyone sells them."

Jace blew out a breath and perched on the edge of the couch. He propped his elbows on his knees and lowered his head, clasping his hands over the back of his neck. "There has to be some way to use this to our advantage."

Maris continued to pace, arms folded across her chest.

"What do you want to do?" Connor leaned a hip against the couch.

Did she really want to run again? Her opinion of Jason Montana had changed drastically since they'd fled Long Island. He was a good man, a strong man, a man who had stepped in front of danger for her more than once, who'd upended his life by running out in the middle of the night to protect a woman he didn't even like. And more than that, she trusted him. The realization came as a shock. When had that happened?

He sat on the couch, seemingly relaxed, though he couldn't possibly be. She had a sudden desire to sit next to him, to absorb some of his strength, his confidence, whatever faith allowed him to remain so strong under such terrifying circumstances. The urge to flee with him battered her.

And yet... The life she'd made for herself hadn't come easy. She'd already walked out on her life twice, first when she'd married Brandon and abandoned all her friends and ambitions, then again by leaving her marriage behind. Divorcing Brandon had been the hardest thing she'd ever done, but she'd gotten through with it. But even after she'd moved on, she'd never gotten close to anyone, holding everyone at arm's length, never allowing herself to trust, to belong. She wanted that sense of belonging, the comfort of being surrounded by people who cared about her. She wanted friends, a family, maybe one day a nice safe husband who didn't have the power to hurt people, didn't wear a mask even in his own home, someone who was anything other than a cop.

Her gaze slid to Jace and she swallowed hard. "I'm going home."

Jace turned a glare on her. "What are you talking about?"

She stood from the chair. This was her decision, not theirs. She'd spent enough of her life doing what other people expected. "I'm exhausted, and I'm going home. I'm tired of running. Besides, what difference does it make? He found me anyway."

Jace stood. "You're not going home."

"Yes. I am. If I run away, he might start killing the victims sooner." She couldn't resist meeting the terror in Maris's eyes. "I'm going back. I'll stop in the garden shop where I first saw the stones as soon as they open and ask if they keep a list of people who bought them. Maybe from credit cards or local customers they remember. Who knows? It might just work."

She wrapped her arms around herself, trying to keep the pieces together. How had her life come to this?

Jace gripped her arms and tilted his head to look into her eyes.

She lifted her gaze to his, ready to argue for what she needed if that was what it took.

Jace's gaze held strong as he studied her. "It can't hurt to try. Maybe the killer bought it and placed it in the intended victim's garden himself. It's not likely he'll be able to find exactly what he needs each time. Chances are he's going to have to create some of the scenes if he wants to continue mimicking them so exactly."

Gratitude poured through her.

He slid a free strand of hair from in front of Addison's face behind her ear.

She tilted her head into his hand, reveling in the warmth and comfort for just a moment. "Thank you."

He cupped her cheek and nodded. "If you insist on going home, I'm going with you."

"So am I. Grab your stuff." Just like Maris. Impatient as always.

The anger she'd felt toward Maris these past years

had already started to dissipate, but it was hard to let go completely, especially when her emotions were so heightened.

Addison started past Maris.

Maris's tentative hand on her arm stopped her.

Addison whirled to face her sister. "What do you want from me? Why are you even here?"

Maris's cheeks reddened. "I've always been here for you, Addison. You were the one who walked away."

"Walked away?" Shock held her tongue for just a moment while the pain of the past clutched her heart. She inhaled deeply, searching for calm, praying for guidance.

"I didn't walk away, Maris. You destroyed my..." She choked on the word *marriage* and couldn't even force it out. "You destroyed me."

"What are you talking about?" Maris shoved her hands into her hair, the large bag slung over her shoulder swinging around and sliding down her arm. She ripped it off her arm and slammed it to the floor. "I've tried to take care of you since you were three."

"I never asked for that."

"You didn't have to. Don't you get it?" Clenching her fists, she took a step toward Addison, bringing them almost nose to nose.

Desperate for air, claustrophobia practically suffocating her, Addison backpedaled, her back slamming into the wall behind her.

"I tried to warn you about Brandon before you married him. I told you what a snake he was even then."

Sweat wormed its way down Addison's back. "I don't want to talk about this right now."

"Of course you don't. You never want to talk about anything unpleasant. You just want to coop yourself up and hide from the world." She shook her head, holding Addison's gaze with her own, then threw her arms in the air and turned away. "It won't work anymore, Addison. It never did."

Seizing the opportunity to get some space, Addison slid away, keeping her back pressed against the wall. She'd managed to distance herself a bit when Maris turned back.

"You have to stop hiding, Addison. From Brandon, from yourself..." Her voice softened. Somehow that was even worse than yelling. "From the truth, from the past."

Addison closed her eyes. Maybe if she ignored Maris, she'd give up and go away.

"I'm not leaving here until we have this conversation." Steel hardened Maris's voice, though she didn't raise it. "If you never want to talk to me again once we're done, that's fine. But you're going to hear me out this time."

Nightmares played through Addison's mind. No, not nightmares. Memories started to surface, but she shoved them away. Pressing a hand against her chest, she tried to relieve the ache. Why was Maris doing this? Addison opened her eyes.

"When you first started dating Brandon, I let it go. I understood you needed to be with someone who made you feel safe, and I was glad he did. But when it became too serious, and he grew more and more controlling and possessive, I got scared." Her breath hitched, and she sniffed.

Addison couldn't do this, couldn't listen to this, couldn't remember what had made her so frightened, so dependent...

"I used some of my contacts at the police station to check around a little, and what I found terrified me."

Jace and Connor stood behind Maris, staring intently at the scene unfolding.

Heat flared in Addison's cheeks. Great. Just what she needed, witnesses to her humiliation.

"Brandon Carlisle is a dirtbag. Half the people who worked under him were terrified of him. The other half were in cahoots with him. He was involved in extortion, bribery, prostitution, gambling… You name it, that creep had a hand in it, all while turning on the charm and appearing to all the world to be a devoted husband and dedicated public servant. And that was then. When I couldn't stop you from marrying him, I kept watching him, waiting patiently for him to make a mistake I could use against him. And when he finally did—"

"I know what he is. Okay? Do you need to hear me say it? Fine. You were right. I needed to feel safe. I needed someone to take care of me." There. She'd admitted it. Now, maybe, Maris would let it go, not force her to dig deeper, to search for the cause. "But I don't anymore. I'm fine now and quite capable of taking care of myself. So leave me be, Maris."

Avoiding Jace's gaze, she turned and stormed across the room. She was going home.

"He killed her, Addison." Maris's words, spoken so softly and with such detachment, stopped her with her hand on the doorknob. "He killed his mistress. And everyone he was involved with knew it. Even those who had been contributing to all of his illegal activities up until that point were shaking in their boots."

Though she desperately wanted to deny the allegation, she couldn't. It was probably true. Though, try as she might, Maris hadn't been able to prove it.

"And he hurt you."

Phantom pain raced across her lower back.

"I know he did. There's no way you fell."

"I'm done, Maris. I don't want to hear any more."

"It's time, Addison."

"No."

"I'm sorry." Sobs wrenched Maris's slim shoulders. "I thought I was doing the right thing, letting you for-get—"

Addison clamped her hands over her ears, a scream welling deep within her.

"It's time to remember, Addison. You were there. You had to have seen—"

"Nooo!"

"I only wanted to protect you. I was a child. I loved you, and I just wanted you with me. You were my sis-ter." Maris crossed the room in three long strides and ripped Addison's hands away from her ears. "I did the wrong thing. I was selfish. I wanted you to stay with me, so I made Daddy take you in. I shouldn't have. They didn't want you there. He and his new wife didn't even want me."

Maris shrugged it off, took a deep shaky breath. "I should have let you go. Maybe if you'd gone into a foster home, they'd have gotten you the therapy you needed, and you wouldn't have ended up where you did."

"You don't understand." With no way to contain her emotions any longer, Addison sobbed.

"I want to."

"You weren't there."

"No. And I'm sorry for that, too. I wanted you to come with me that weekend, and you were supposed to, but you backed out at the last minute. I should have stayed home with you. If I hadn't been with my father that weekend—"

Addison held her hands out in front of her and backed

up. She had to get away. "Please stop, Maris. I can't do this. Not right now. Please."

Maris held her gaze for a long time, searching for something in Addison's expression. Whatever she found, she relented. Her shoulders slumped and she nodded. "Okay. Only for now, though."

"Fine." Relief weakened her knees and they threatened to give out. "We can talk about it another time."

"Sure."

"I need to lie down for a few minutes." She turned her back on the three of them.

Their hushed voices faded as they retreated through the connecting door to Jace's room, but she ignored them, flopped onto the bed and covered her head with a pillow. As long as the past stayed buried, she didn't really care what they thought.

Jace closed the door, leaving it ajar in case Addison needed help. He could only give her a few minutes to recover before they had to go. He turned to Maris. "You said something about Addison staying behind one weekend when she was supposed to go somewhere with you. What's the significance of that?"

Maris tilted her head. "What? No questions about Brandon murdering his mistress?"

He peeked out between the curtain, scanning the courtyard, then returned his focus to her. "Nope."

Brandon's mistress had been found stabbed to death in a hotel room. But even if the knife wounds hadn't killed her, the overdose she'd taken most likely would have. The overdose the investigating detectives had suspected was caused by drugs Brandon had provided, though they couldn't find a way to prove it. Since Maris's article came out soon after that, Jace had already been on his way out by the time the investigation got underway and hadn't been privy to much of the information. But he wouldn't share any of that with Maris. It was none of her business.

She stared at him a few seconds longer, then flopped into an armchair, sighed and propped her feet on the ottoman.

"I can't protect her, or you, if I don't know what's going on."

"I'm not worried about being protected." She huffed out a breath and dropped her head back, closing her eyes. "And I've been protecting my sister most of my life."

"Protecting her from what?"

Connor cleared his throat, interrupting before Jace could say anything else. Probably a good thing, since anything he said now would only lead to an argument.

Jace started toward the connecting door. It was time to go.

"Does this have anything to do with the woman who was murdered thirty years ago?" Connor's question stopped Jace dead in his tracks.

He held his breath, afraid of missing her answer.

Maris sat up straighter. "Were you able to find any public records on that?"

"While looking for similarities between past crimes and the murders that have already taken place, one of my researchers found an old newspaper article. Apparently, the case about thirty years ago closely mirrored the recent ones."

Jace turned back to them. "But that doesn't make sense. Addison's book only came out last year."

"Exactly." Connor nodded and focused on Maris. "Tell him."

She blew out a breath and then spoke so softly it was hard to make out what she was saying. "She was supposed to go with me to my father's that weekend. But she was going through a phase where she was very attached to our mother. At the last minute, she started crying she didn't want to go."

Jace moved closer.

"I thought about staying home with her, but I was angry, and maybe a little jealous that she wanted to stay home with Mother instead of coming with me." She shook her head and sobbed softly.

Jace wanted to push her for answers, but Connor shook his head, so Jace waited her out.

"Our mother was murdered." Her shoulders slumped with the admission. "Addison was three, and the only witness. At least I think she was a witness."

"The article mentioned a child being found at the scene, but her name was withheld because she was a minor," Connor added.

Jace couldn't stay still any longer. "Did they catch the killer?"

She shook her head. "But our older brother and his father both disappeared at the same time. The police figured his father killed our mother and kidnapped Eddie. It was big news for a while, but then it faded as more urgent stories took its place. You know how it is."

"Wait a minute." Questions ricocheted through his head. "Why hasn't Addison ever mentioned any of this?"

Maris took a shaky breath and studied him for a moment. "She doesn't talk about it. Ever. Hasn't since the day it happened."

Jace patted his pockets, but he had no pad or pen to take notes. He rifled through a small desk in the corner and came up with a sheet of printer paper and a pen. He laid the paper on the desk, leaned over and started jotting notes. "Were they ever found?"

"Eddie's father turned up dead about ten years ago. It was ruled a suspicious death. Eddie was never found."

"All three of you had different fathers?"

"Yes."

"How old was your brother when he disappeared?"

"Fifteen."

"Did he live with you?"

"Yes."

"Did he want to live with his father?"

"I have no idea. I was only eight at the time."

"Did Addison actually see her get killed?"

"She's never said." Maris sighed. "Addison's father had already passed away, and I wanted her to stay with me, so after our mother was killed, my father took custody of her. But like I said, he didn't want her, and he only did the bare minimum. He fed her, kept a roof over her head…that's about it. He didn't even buy her clothes. I passed mine down to her. When I turned eighteen, I moved out and took her with me." She finally sat back down on the chair. "We'd never discussed what happened, but I tried to get her into therapy once I moved out. She refused. When I dragged her there, she clamped her mouth closed and wouldn't say a word. But she suffered horrible nightmares after the murder. I have a feeling she saw the whole thing."

"What makes you say that?" Jace held the pen poised over the paper.

"The police found her hiding in a cabinet. They called my father right away to make sure I was with him. I pitched a fit until he went and picked up Addison." Maris twisted her hands together, twining and untwining her fingers. "Once I became a journalist, I had a friend in the department copy the case file." She jumped up and started to pace. "Including the crime scene photos."

"And?"

She stopped and faced Jace, holding his gaze. "I always thought she witnessed the murder, but when I read her book, there was no doubt. The first murder scene matches the crime scene exactly. My mother's murder could have taken place exactly as Addison described it in the book."

Connor stood behind his wife, gently massaging her shoulders. "Did you ever ask her if she saw what happened?"

"Of course."

"And she denied it?"

Maris shrugged him off and paced. "She avoided answering. Every time."

Connor stepped into her path, blocking her forward progress. "Thank you, Maris. I know it couldn't have been easy for you to relive that."

She shrugged and lowered her gaze. "But does it help?"

"Yes." Jace studied his notes, leaving Connor to comfort his wife. Did her admission help him? Probably. Information usually did, though he couldn't quite figure out how yet. "One more thing."

"What?"

"Did you know Eddie's father? Did he seem like the violent type to you?"

"I don't know. I was only eight…" She frowned. "But I don't ever remember feeling afraid of him. I only met him a few times, but he seemed all right, I guess. Why?"

Something was bugging him, though he couldn't

place his finger on exactly what it was. "The first murder in Addison's book was an excessively violent scene. A man not prone to violence… I don't know."

Connor ignored the rising anger in Jace's tone. "A crime of passion, maybe?"

"Maybe." Jace had to concede. Crimes committed in the heat of the moment could be particularly violent. He pointed the pen at Connor. "Brandon Carlisle would have had access to the file on Addison's mother's murder."

"True." Connor nodded. "But he also could have read the book, so that really doesn't prove anything."

Phoenix scrambled to his feet, his deep bark echoing through the small space, and lunged toward the door that led outside.

No way was the killer getting anywhere near Addison. Jace reached for his gun.

TEN

Raised voices drifted to her.

Addison hurried to the connecting door.

It swung open before she could grab it, and she jumped back.

Jace gripped her arm. "Addison, stay calm."

"Stay…what?"

Two cops strode through the door. "Mrs. Carlisle?"

"No." She hadn't gone by that name in more than three years, and she wasn't about to answer to it now.

The young cop hesitated and glanced at his even-younger-looking partner, who only shrugged, then turned his attention back to her. "You're not Addison Carlisle?"

Jace's face was almost purple, his gun nowhere to be seen.

Sweat dripped a steady line down her back. "Not anymore."

The urge to flee hammered her. Claustrophobia held her trapped in place.

The cop's frown deepened. "Come with me, please."

Jace snaked an arm around her shoulders, leaning close to whisper, "Do what they say. I'll be right behind you."

Addison reeled.

Keeping his arm firmly in place, Jace faced the two cops. "I already told you, we'll bring her in for questioning. Her attorney is being contacted as we speak. She'll come in with him and answer any questions you have."

"I'm sorry, sir, but a warrant has been issued, and my orders are to take her into custody."

He dropped his arm and stepped in front of her. "She's being arrested? On what grounds?"

"Obstruction of justice. She will be extradited back to Long Island shortly, into SCPD custody. A sheriff is already on his way."

She had to get out of there. She took a step backward.

Jace tensed. "Please, Addison. Don't do this."

She had to run.

He held both of her arms and squeezed, staring into her eyes. While his were filled with concern, she didn't sense any actual fear. Of course, he had nothing to be afraid of. He wouldn't end up dead if he went with these cops. "We'll be right behind you. Connor is on the phone with a lawyer right now. He'll take care of it. Please. Trust me."

Trust him? He had to be kidding. She hadn't trusted anyone in more years than she could remember, and look what had happened when she'd lowered her guard the smallest bit, when she'd allowed Jace to worm his way beneath her defenses. Lowering her gaze in defeat, she only nodded.

Jace released her and stepped back.

One of the cops moved toward her.

Her breath caught, pressure building in her chest, but she refused to give in to the tears clogging her throat. No way would she give Brandon's cronies the satisfaction.

"Is that really necessary?" Jace gestured toward the handcuffs the officer held.

A touch of pink tinged his freckled cheeks. "Sorry, sir. She already ran from the authorities on Long Island, and I was instructed to cuff her."

Jace stepped between her and the officer. "First of all, she didn't run from anyone. Second of all, if she was hiding, how'd you know where to find her?"

He blushed deeper. "Anonymous tip."

So the killer had followed them. Her breath hitched, but she still swallowed the sobs begging for release and reached for Jace's hand.

He gripped hers and squeezed. "Don't worry, I'll be right behind you, and Connor will catch up as soon as he makes a few calls and one of his guys picks them up."

"Turn around, please, ma'am." The cop gripped her arm and read her Miranda rights.

Addison turned and held her shaking hands behind her back while the cop cuffed her. Heaving in slow, deep breaths, she struggled against nausea.

The two cops fell into step on either side of her, leading her toward the door, forcing Jace to follow behind them.

Phoenix stood alert, blocking the door. He growled low in his throat, the sound even more threatening because it was so quiet.

Though Connor's back faced her as he looked over the deck railing, phone pressed to his ear, his stiff posture told her he wasn't happy with whatever he was hearing. A quick scan of the room as she crossed brought no sign of Maris.

A cool breeze fluttered her hair as the cops ushered her through the doorway to the waiting police cruiser. Dried leaves skittered across the courtyard. She inhaled deeply, dragging the crisp, fall air into her lungs before one of the cops pressed a hand to the top of her head and guided her into the back seat.

Addison turned and looked out the back window.

Leaving Phoenix with Connor, Jace jumped into Connor's new car and slammed the door. He pulled out behind them and stayed glued to the patrol car's bumper.

Knowing he was behind her brought a small glimmer of hope. Maybe he'd be able to keep her from falling into Brandon's hands. Probably not, but if nothing else, he'd try to make sure Brandon was punished if she disappeared. That knowledge offered a surprising measure of comfort.

She tried to find relief in that, but her mind couldn't focus on anything but the gut-wrenching fear that had become her constant companion since she'd received the first email from the killer.

A chill tore through her as they hurtled down the highway with the lights flashing and the siren blaring— a completely unnecessary show of power on the deserted highway, probably engineered to instill fear in their captive. It wouldn't work. Not even Brandon frightened her more than the killer she'd unwittingly unleashed on the unsuspecting public…on her own sister. Although, who knew? Maybe they were one and the same.

A bump jarred her from the guilt as the cruiser jostled her on its way into the small parking lot of the Shady Creek Police Department. The early Saturday morning quiet was interrupted only by birds chirping happily in the trees, the occasional bark of a dog in the distance and children's laughter as a group of young boys on bicycles cut across the parking lot, one of them jumping off the curb and launching his bike into the street.

The deceptively peaceful illusion was shattered by the Suffolk County sheriff's car, used to transport prisoners, sitting in the far corner. Two deputies leaned against the hood, arms folded across their chests, faces schooled in expressions meant to intimidate.

The two Shady Creek officers shared a look, innocence apparent in their youthful but concerned expressions, and handed her over to the deputies with a small stack of paperwork, few pleasantries and no conversation. They stared after her as she was escorted to the waiting sheriff's car.

Jace remained in Connor's car, parked on the side of the road behind a blue SUV.

With no move to take off the handcuffs, the deputies guided her into the back of the car.

She leaned against the seat as best she could with her hands cuffed behind her back and settled in for the long trip to Long Island. Dropping her head against the seat, she let her eyes drift closed, the smooth rocking motion lulling her, allowing her mind to wander.

She'd written her first novel in an attempt to alleviate the nightmares that had plagued her childhood, harassed her through her teenage years and pursued her into adulthood. The woman sprawled in the middle of the kitchen, blood spattered on the wood cabinets, her long, dark hair swimming in an ever-growing pool of red so deep it was almost black.

Though her face had been turned away, there was something familiar about her. Addison should know who the woman was. Dream Addison, a combination of the child she'd been and the adult she was now, crept closer, reaching out to smooth a clean section of hair.

The child and the adult battled in her mind, the adult Addison begging the child to retreat, the child insisting on knowing the truth. The child's hand hovered over the woman, about to—

The car door whipped open, and a rough hand reached in, grabbed her arm and dragged her from the back seat.

They'd reached Long Island, and Jace still hadn't heard from Connor. He gripped the steering wheel tighter, his knuckles white with the strain. Where in the world was Connor with the lawyer? One of the deputies slammed the car door closed behind Addison and shoved her toward the police station. She stumbled, and he released her as she fell, hands cuffed behind her back. At the last minute, she was able to twist and cushion the fall with her injured shoulder instead of landing on her face.

Forget waiting for Connor. He jumped out of the car, locked the door, then pocketed the keys. No way was he going to sit there and wait for a lawyer while the deputies mistreated Addison, no matter what Connor's instructions had been.

He jogged across the small parking lot toward them.

One of the deputies had gone ahead and now stood beside the door. The other propped a hand on his holstered weapon and waited for Addison to struggle to her feet.

She stood, chin lifted in defiance, and met the deputy's gaze before turning and walking into the police station, the door falling shut behind her as Jace reached the sidewalk.

Ringing from his cell phone made him pause long enough to pull the phone from his pocket and check the caller ID. Connor. Finally. Then he resumed his pursuit. "Where's the lawyer?"

The hiss of static from the bad connection cut off the start of Connor's reply. "...his way."

"What? You're breaking up." He stopped, torn between following Addison and talking to Connor. The only one who could help her now was the lawyer. He stared after Addison, then moved away from the building to get better service.

"...be there...meet..."

Jace pressed a hand against his free ear and held the phone tighter against the other in an effort to decipher the words interspersed between crackles and hums. "I can't make out what you're saying. Where do I have to meet him?"

"Front door."

Scanning the parking lot in search of anyone who might be waiting, Jace ignored the noise of the connection and whatever else Connor was trying to say. A woman in a business suit strode toward him, briefcase swinging at her side, then continued into the building without slowing.

He pulled the phone from his ear and glanced at the screen. Call failed. Clutching the phone in a grip tight enough to crush it, he shoved it into his pocket, whatever Connor had been trying to say lost in the electronic haze of faulty cell phone connections.

A slightly disheveled man, wearing slacks and a button-down shirt with the sleeves rolled up and the collar open, paused on the top step, turned and looked around. He lifted a hand as Jace approached. "Jace Montana?"

"Yes." He shook the proffered hand.

"Austin Lowe." He held the door open for Jace to precede him and spoke while he strode through the lobby. "Connor asked me to meet you. His cell phone service was bad, but he said you'd bring me up to date."

Austin dropped his briefcase onto the belt beside the metal detector, fished his keys from his pocket and tossed them behind the briefcase, then walked through the metal detector. Apparently, Connor had managed to convey the urgency of the situation, if nothing else.

Jace followed him unimpeded, then waited while Austin surveyed the directory posted on the wall beside the elevators.

"Second floor." Instead of waiting for the elevator, he jogged up the stairs.

Jace brought him up to speed as much as possible, relaying all of the information he had so far.

The two deputies who'd transported Addison emerged from a doorway at the end of the hall and strolled toward them. The one who'd shoved Addison laughed at something the other said. "...Niagara Falls this weekend with Courtney and the kids."

Jace angled himself toward the offender. When he came within striking distance, Jace bumped him with his shoulder, hard.

The deputy stepped back, met Jace's harsh glare and tipped his hat. "Sorry, man, gotta look where I'm going." He kept walking.

Austin continued down the hallway without breaking stride and entered the doorway the two men had just left.

Jace followed, catching the door before it could close all the way, then met Austin at the counter.

The lawyer was already trying to get a woman's attention. "Excuse me."

"Just a minute, please." A harried-looking clerk

rushed past, carrying a stack of folders, and disappeared through a doorway at the side of the room.

Austin stroked a hand over his goatee, then rapped his knuckles against the bulletproof glass, craning his neck to see past the partitions dividing the office into cubicles.

The clatter of fingers flying over a keyboard, music playing quietly and muffled voices assured Jace there were more people hiding back there than just the one clerk. He didn't have the time or the patience to wait for her to come back. He turned the knob and shoved against the door that led to the work area. Nothing. Locked up tight.

The clerk hurried back into the room and disappeared behind a maroon partition.

Austin scrolled through his phone.

Fed up, Jace fisted his hand and pounded against the window. "Hey."

When the woman poked her head around the corner, he gestured her forward.

"Yes?" She approached the window tentatively, as if scared he'd launch himself through the glass. Her assessment wasn't far off. "Can I help you gentlemen?"

Stuffing the phone into his pocket, Austin smiled. "Yes, ma'am. Please. I'm Addison Keller's attorney."

The woman's frown only fueled Jace's anger.

"You'll have to give me a minute." She started to move away again.

"Look, ma'am." Austin pressed a hand against Jace's chest, restraining any outburst, and leaned toward the woman. "My client was just brought in for questioning, and I must see her."

"Have a seat, and I'll find out where she is."

He nodded and turned on Jace while the woman disappeared through the door once more. "I know you're frustrated, but that woman has the power to make us wait a long time. Why don't you step outside and calm down?"

Confident the defense attorney would get to Addison, probably faster without Jace hindering him, Jace shoved through the doorway. Pacing the hallway, he kept a close eye on Austin. He'd call Connor and give the other man until he got off the phone to make it past the woman guarding the desk before he turned this place upside down in search of her.

Connor picked up on the fourth ring. "Yeah."

"The lawyer's here, but one of the clerks is blocking him."

"Don't worry about it. He'll get in."

"How can you be sure?"

Silence greeted him.

"Fine." Not wanting to waste the decent cell phone connection, he let it go. "Have you found out anything about the anonymous tip that led to them finding Addison?"

"Yes and no."

The clerk came back, waving animatedly while Austin nodded.

Fear for Addison's safety shortened his temper. "What's that supposed to mean?"

"A call came in about forty minutes after we left the cabin." He turned away or covered the phone to speak to someone in the background, his muffled voice coming through the receiver, but Jace couldn't make out the words. "Just long enough for the killer to have followed us to the motel, then reach somewhere with decent cell phone service and make the call."

"You think Brandon Carlisle is involved?"

"Either that, or the killer's done his research and knows about Addison's history with Brandon and the SCPD, and knows she wouldn't receive a warm welcome."

Frustration tormented him. "Where are you?"

"I'm headed out that way. At least I'm out of the mountains now, so my cell phone should work. I'll call you back when I get closer."

As Jace turned to look at Austin, the lawyer placed both hands flat against the counter, leaning close enough to press his nose against the bulletproof glass, his posture rigid. All signs of the easygoing man with the ready smile had disappeared.

"Gotta go." He ended the call and stuffed the phone into his pocket, then went to see what the problem was.

ELEVEN

Addison kept her back rigid, careful not to slouch in the hard, metal chair, refusing to bend under Detective Marshall Brooks's harsh stare. She worked to ignore the disapproval in his scowl and kept her voice calm. "I already told you. I wasn't trying to evade the police. I was scared, and I wanted to get away for a little while. And that's all I'm going to say without my attorney present."

The heavyset detective leaned forward, hands splayed on the table, anger turning his already ruddy complexion even redder.

She would never turn her gaze away first. When they'd offered her a phone call, she'd declined, thinking Connor was already making arrangements. Maybe she shouldn't have. But who would she have called anyway, a random attorney she chose from the yellow pages?

"So you climbed out the window in the middle of the night?"

Silence.

"Why?"

She could just explain, tell him she thought someone was in the house, but it probably wouldn't matter anyway. The fact that Detective Brooks was still hammering her with questions after she'd requested her attorney told her all she needed to know about his association with Brandon. Better to wait until she spoke to a lawyer.

"...pictures?"

Uh-oh. What had he said? Lulled by the repetitive line of questioning, she hadn't paid enough attention. "I'm sorry?"

He lifted a brow with just the right amount of derision evident in the expression, and she couldn't help but wonder if he practiced the skeptical look in front of the mirror. "I said, how do you explain the pictures?"

"Pictures?" A line of sweat snaked its way down her back. "What pictures?"

"The pictures of the crime scene on your computer."

Oh, no. She'd forgotten about the emails, forgotten her computer would have been sitting on her bed, open, when the police had come to search for her. Had they searched the house?

Hopefully, Connor would come through with a lawyer in a hurry.

The detective paced the small area in front of the table, hands clasped behind his back, hard expression reflected in what she figured was a two-way mirror each time he turned, then changed tactics. "Sales of your book certainly have increased in the past couple of days."

A small glimmer of happiness tried to surface as it always did at the prospect people were enjoying her book, but it dimmed instantly when she realized why sales had increased.

"Just in time for the second installment." He stopped pacing and stood facing her, then leaned forward deliberately, flattening his hands against the table, caging her gaze with his. "That's quite a coincidence."

The breath shot from her lungs as if she'd been sucker

punched. He couldn't possibly think… Of course, thinking he had evidence of her guilt would certainly explain his attitude. "I need to use the ladies' room."

"As soon as we're done here."

"No. Now."

He glanced pointedly at his watch. "You know, it's still early enough to get you before a judge for arraignment if you talk now, tell us what's really going on. Might keep you from spending the night in jail."

She pushed her chair back and stood, rubbing her wrists where the handcuffs had chafed. "It was a long trip, and I need to use the restroom."

The detective glanced at his partner, who'd remained quietly in his chair this whole time, and shrugged as if it didn't matter. He opened the door. "Come with me."

The suspicion that he'd given in too easily rode her as he escorted her down the hallway, his partner falling into step on her other side. The detective pushed open the bathroom door and gestured her inside. He and his partner took up positions on either side of the door, their backs to the hallway wall.

Addison let the door fall shut then turned and leaned against it, thankful for the moment of solitude. She'd become too used to being alone and was never quite comfortable in the presence of others, especially anyone wearing a uniform or carrying a badge. Any plan of escape fell flat in the windowless room. Probably for the best, anyway.

What she really needed was a hot bubble bath and a cup of coffee, maybe a little something to eat.

She scoffed. More likely she'd end up with a cot and a toilet in a five-by-eight cage.

She shoved away from the door.

She couldn't imagine where Jace was. She'd been

right to trust him. God had answered her prayers when He'd sent Jason Montana to save her. But one man could only do so much.

How had she ended up in this mess? She stared into the mirror above the sinks and a stranger stared back at her. An older woman than she remembered, with disheveled hair, dark circles ringing her eyes and a pallid complexion. Fear. Fear had dictated every step she'd taken so far. From the day Maris had forced her to realize the truth of what a monster she'd married, fear had ruled her. Enough. It was time to stand up and face this instead of running away.

A sob escaped, and she struggled to stifle the sound. No need for the detectives standing outside the door to know they'd upset her. She washed her hands, then tied her long hair back in a knot, closed her eyes and splashed blessedly cool water over her face. Keeping her head lowered, she let the water drip into the sink.

Someone extended a wad of paper towels from the dispenser into her line of vision. Funny, she hadn't heard anyone come in. Then again, she'd been so flustered she hadn't bothered to check the stalls. She took the paper towels. "Thank y—"

A strong hand clamped over her mouth and another gripped the back of her hair and yanked her upright, turning her toward him. Brandon pulled her face closer to his until they were almost nose to nose. "Hello, Addison."

She froze, too terrified to even struggle.

His hushed laughter echoed through the empty room. He squeezed her face, the pressure of his fingers threatening to crush her cheekbones. "Imagine meeting you here."

Deliver me from evil. Stand with me. Lend me Your strength. Oh, Lord, help me.

She heaved in a deep breath through her nose, the air thick with the stench of his overly sweet cologne, and schooled her features, knowing the flat expression was the least likely to provoke him.

"When I remove my hand, you will not scream. Do you understand?"

She nodded slowly, careful to keep her gaze averted.

He released her slowly, hesitant, as if afraid she'd go back on her word. Maybe the two cops stationed outside the door didn't know he was in here. The thought of screaming for help slipped quickly through her mind and right back out again. If the two detectives were in cahoots with him, she'd most likely disappear.

Brandon looked perfect, as always. Not one slick black hair out of place, his suit impeccably pressed, his expression a mask of control. But she knew what lurked beneath the deceptive exterior. A monster, his temper quick and fierce.

She kept her voice low. "How'd you know I'd be here?"

Not that it mattered, but someone had to have told him where to find her, and very few people knew. The killer among them.

"Really? With your nerves? As soon as I got word you'd been picked up, it was a given you'd end up in the bathroom blubbering like an idiot."

She ignored the dig. His opinion of her had stopped mattering long ago. "What do you want?"

"Answers."

"Answers to what?"

He turned at the sound of raised voices in the hallway.

The bathroom door swung open, slamming into the wall behind it with enough force to rattle the mirror.

* * *

Jace left the lawyer in the hallway to battle it out with the two detectives and strode through the bathroom doorway ready for a fight. One quick glance assured him Addison was shaken but okay. Bruises on her cheekbones—amid the scabbed-over scratches and cuts from their flight through the woods—fueled his anger. When he turned on Brandon Carlisle, years of pent-up frustration and rage surged through him.

He prayed for self-control. "What are you doing here?"

Brandon grinned, a calculated look Jace had observed too many times for it to have any effect on him. "Well, hello there, Jace. What brings you here? Decided to join me after all?"

Jace loosened his clenched fists and ignored the taunt.

Brandon smoothed his jacket and ran a hand over his hair. Nervous gestures were unusual for the Brandon Jace remembered. "I can get you back on the force in a heartbeat, you know."

"I don't want anything from you." Though he desperately wanted to return to his former career, if God meant for him to be back on the force, he'd be there. Of course, the well of self-pity he'd fallen into would have kept that from happening even if it had been meant for him. Even God couldn't help him if he refused to cooperate, refused to help himself.

"Oh, that's right. Well, if you don't want anything from me, what are you doing here?" He stole a glance at Addison and frowned when he turned back to Jace. Twin spots of red flared on his cheeks. "Unless maybe there was something you wanted from me all along. Tell me, Jace, is that why you wouldn't accept my offer, wouldn't join me and my men? Did you have a thing for my wife?"

Typical of Brandon, always believing there had to be an ulterior motive. He couldn't accept that Jace had no interest in doing anything illegal, or even immoral. Everything this man did was self-serving, so he couldn't understand how other people could put someone else ahead of themselves, could sacrifice their own needs or desires for those of others.

Brandon turned on Addison. "Imagine finding my wife with my sworn enemy."

Addison averted her gaze as she shook her head. "I'm not your wife."

Brandon took a step toward her and lifted his hand.

Jace intercepted him, catching Brandon's arm mid-swing. He shoved Brandon back against the wall, willing him to stay there so he could get Addison to safety without having to hurt him.

Brandon's head smacked against the tile with a resounding and satisfying thud. He hurled himself back at Jace, hitting him hard with a shoulder into his gut. He wrapped his arms around Jace's waist and propelled him backward.

Moving with the momentum, Jace backpedaled and turned, throttling Brandon's head and shoulder into the tiled wall behind him.

"Stop it!" Addison's scream barely penetrated the haze of rage clouding his mind and judgment.

But it penetrated enough to make him release his hold and step back.

Brandon came again.

"That's enough. You're drawing too much attention now." The two detectives grabbed Brandon's arms and wrestled him back across the room. One of them whirled on Jace. "What are you doing in here?"

"Me?" As if the arrogant loser had every right to be standing in a women's restroom tormenting his ex-wife.

Jace surged toward him.

Austin stepped into his path, barring the way. He blocked Jace and leaned close. "Let it go, man. Right now, he's got a lot to answer for."

Jace swallowed hard, trying desperately to rein in the fear that had overtaken him when he'd found Brandon with Addison. While he might have some hope of controlling his anger, the fear threatened to consume him.

The lawyer shoved Jace back and kept him pinned with his gaze. Keeping a firm hand against Jace's chest, he gestured Addison toward the door. "Come on, Addison."

She hurried out.

The two detectives had Brandon caged in the far corner, voices pitched low in what sounded like an argument.

Jace shoved away from the wall, keeping his glare on Brandon, letting him know this wasn't over by a long shot.

When Brandon smiled, flashing his overly white teeth, Austin grabbed Jace none too gently by the arm and propelled him out the doorway. "Think about this, Jace. He doesn't matter right now. What matters is getting Addison before a judge and out of here and somewhere safe. That's your job, and you can't do it from a cell."

The reality of the statement dispersed some of the mental fog, bringing him back from the brink. Sweat broke out on his forehead, all the spit dried up in his mouth and his hands trembled. He had to get out of there. With a hand against the small of Addison's back, he guided her down the hallway. Brandon should already be cuffed and on his way to jail. The fact he wasn't meant that either the detectives were on his payroll, which was likely, or he was about to sweet-talk his way out of trouble. Again. They had to find a way to get her out of there before that happened.

Austin increased his pace, and Jace and Addison sped up beside him.

"Where are we going?" Not that it mattered, as long as it was away from there.

"She's going before the judge for arraignment." He shot Jace a pointed look. "Then you're going to get her out of here."

They took the stairs up one more floor, entered the small courtroom, and Jace slid into the empty first row while Addison and Austin stood before the judge, who was already seated at the bench, apparently waiting. Someone definitely knew how to get things done. If not the lawyer, Connor probably had a hand in her quick arraignment.

Austin stood before the judge and explained the situation, arguing that Addison hadn't fled but simply gone somewhere she felt was safe when she feared she was in danger.

"I've gone over the paperwork. Is there anything you'd like to add?" Shuffling through the papers on his desk, the judge peered over his glasses at Addison.

She glanced at Austin, who shook his head.

"Very well. You are being charged with obstruction of justice for impeding the progress of an investigation. In light of your attorney's argument that you didn't actually flee from the police, but in fear for your life…"

And the fact they had no legitimate reason to arrest her.

"I'm releasing you on your own recognizance. But…"

Addison sucked in a breath and opened her mouth, but a nudge from the lawyer stayed her response.

"Only on the condition you remain on Long Island and available to answer questions and cooperate fully with the investigation." He stared her down, obviously waiting for some sort of response.

Addison's posture stiffened. "Yes, Your Honor."

While Austin agreed to the terms and made arrangements for her release, Jace kept most of his attention on Addison.

An air of defeat surrounded her as she turned, her lower lip trembling, and headed toward him on her way out of the courtroom.

He slid into the aisle behind her and grabbed Austin's arm as they followed her out. "What's going on, man? Obstruction? You've got to be kidding me."

"Doesn't matter." Austin waved him off. He pushed through the doorway to the parking lot and held it open for them to pass. "Just get out of here before they change their minds. I'll call Connor and update him."

Addison stopped and faced Austin, then extended a hand. "I don't know how to thank you."

"You're welcome." He smiled warmly and shook her hand. "Now go, get out of here."

Jace jogged down the stairs, staying behind Addison, just in case Brandon managed to free himself of the two detectives before they made it to the car.

"And make sure Connor knows where to find you," Austin called after them.

Jace pulled his keys from his pocket and hit the unlock button, then opened the door and guided Addison inside.

Taking a few deep breaths of the cool air, Jace rounded the car and surveyed the parking lot before slipping in beside Addison. Too focused on getting a grip on his own emotions, Jace let her be while he started the car and sped down the road.

She remained silent until he hit the highway. "Thank you."

"No problem." His mouth felt like it was filled with paste, and his tongue stuck to the roof of his mouth when he tried to talk. Spotting a McDonald's, he pulled through the drive-through. "Want anything?"

"A Diet Coke, please."

Once he got their sodas, he pulled to a far corner of the parking lot where he'd be able to keep an eye on both entrances, backed into a spot beneath a large oak tree, opened the windows and turned off the ignition. He needed a minute to collect himself.

When Austin and he had approached the two detectives in the hallway and Austin had started questioning them, Jace had pressed his ear against the bathroom door. He didn't have to recognize the muffled sound of a man's voice coming from the other side to know who it belonged to.

The intensity of his feelings for Addison had sucker punched him; the thought of anything happening to her had been more than he could take. He'd desperately wanted to destroy Brandon, then wrap her in his embrace, shelter her from harm, cocoon her in warmth and safety, protect her.

He couldn't deny the depth of his feelings for her, feelings that might have progressed slower had he not been so afraid for her safety. Feelings that might once have mattered, if he desired or deserved a relationship. As it was, the rush of emotions had blindsided him, and the power of the emotions that tore through him had driven him into that bathroom without even a single thought for his own safety.

And he'd prayed, the words that had once eluded him coming easily when the plea had been for Addison and not himself.

"I'm sorry." Her quiet apology pulled him back to reality. The bruises on her cheek were already darkening. She frowned. "I wasn't sure I believed you. I didn't understand why you'd resign if you weren't involved in what was going on with Brandon."

He appreciated the fact she wasn't asking, but rather letting him decide if he wanted to share anything without making him feel obligated. His hand shook, rattling the ice as he lifted the large soda and sucked half of it down, the receding adrenaline surge leaving him edgy. Caffeine and sugar might not have been the best choice. Water would probably have been better. "After Maris's article, which is when I first learned Brandon was anything other than what he appeared to be, I couldn't bring myself to trust anyone. Some of my fellow officers were only involved because they had no other options, had families to support, children to feed. Brandon threatened them, and they had too much to lose to stand up to him."

"Brandon preys on people like that. He finds their weaknesses and exploits them. He knows they won't have the resources or the energy to cross him."

"Exactly." He let his head fall back against the headrest. "And I didn't know who to trust. No one does. That's part of the problem. It could be, and probably is, only a handful of people are directly involved in Brandon's activities. But who do you trust? How do you do the job not knowing who has your back?"

She couldn't give him answers. No one could. Which was why he'd chosen to resign, to simply walk away from a career he loved.

He ran his thumb over the bruise on her cheek, careful not to apply too much pressure. "He hit you?"

"No." She shook her head and shifted her gaze, but he cupped her cheek and brought her focus back to him. "He just squeezed my face. It's no big deal."

"He shouldn't have put his hands on you." And next time he did, Jace would—

She covered his hand with her own. "I'm fine. I'm just sorry I involved you in this."

"You didn't involve me, Connor did." He grinned. Odd to realize he was no longer sorry for his involvement. He should have taken on Brandon Carlisle long ago.

"But now you're on Brandon's radar, and the killer's radar, and it's my fault. I'm sorry I didn't clear up that you and I weren't…involved. The accusation caught me off guard."

He skimmed his fingers along the bruises Brandon's fingers had left. The depth of the vulnerability pooled in her green eyes called to him. A wave of feelings he couldn't understand rushed through him, and he leaned toward her.

The ring of his cell phone stopped him short. He swallowed hard, forcing down the heightened emotions the encounter had brought to the surface and the knowledge she was being hunted by a killer, and answered the call. "Yeah, Connor, I have her."

Addison leaned back against the car door. Retreating from him?

"Austin called." Connor's voice pulled his attention from her. "Said you had a run-in with Brandon."

"Yeah. Unfortunately, I didn't run into him hard enough to tumble him off his high horse."

"Don't worry about him. When this is over, we'll take him down. We have faith in you, Jace, Maris and I both. And we'll do everything in our power to help put an end to Brandon Carlisle's influence."

Jace had every intention of doing just that, and while he appreciated the sentiment and the feeling evident in Connor's voice, when the time came, Brandon Carlisle belonged to him.

TWELVE

Addison jogged up the front steps, grateful to be home. She stopped at the crime scene tape that had been strung across the closed door.

"Austin said they're done here. You can go ahead in." Jace stood behind her, a little too close for comfort, even though he was only trying to protect her.

"It's not that." She stepped back.

"Then what's wrong? We don't want to stand out here any longer than necessary."

"When I left…" Had it really only been the night before last? "I didn't take anything with me. I don't have the key."

Jace reached past her, pulled down the crime scene tape, turned the knob and pushed the door open.

Nice. They couldn't even lock the front door.

Once she'd moved into the foyer and closed the front door, Jace held out a hand to stop her. "Wait here with Phoenix."

Surely the dog would have alerted them if anyone waited in the house? Weaving her fingers into Phoenix's fur, she waited for Jace to search the house. Exhaustion beat at her.

Phoenix sat in the middle of the hallway, his presence bringing her comfort. She was glad Connor had dropped him off to them, even though he'd had to meet with someone and couldn't stay.

A trip to the shelter for a dog of her own was definitely in order. She was tired of being alone, of keeping her head down, of being afraid to trust anyone.

She pressed a hand against her face where Jace's fingers had brushed her skin. The bruises left by Brandon, though a little tender, didn't bother her. It was the phantom touch of Jace's fingers still lingering against her cheek that had her heart racing. Heat flamed her cheeks.

"All clear."

"Thank you." She started past him toward the stairs. "I just need to grab my cell phone and computer."

"Mind if I tag along?"

Did she? "Sure."

He followed her up the stairs and into her room.

Everything was pretty much as she remembered leaving it, except for her computer, which was missing. Apparently, the police had confiscated it after the killer had saved the pictures to her hard drive. It could have been worse. She'd expected the house would be trashed. They must have been content to find evidence they could use against her.

The tea that had spilled across the nightstand and run down its side in a sticky mess would most likely leave a permanent stain on the light wood.

Addison smoothed her long hair away from her face, plucked an elastic band from her nightstand and tied her hair back. "If you'll excuse me, please, I have to get this mess cleaned up so I can lie down. I'm exhausted."

She turned her back to him and righted the cup.

Jace picked up the comforter balled up on the floor and tossed it onto the bed.

She plucked her cell phone out of a puddle of dried tea on the floor and tried to wipe it off with a tissue. They'd left it sitting in the mess. She pressed the button, and her home screen popped right up.

Only 4 percent charge left. She'd have to plug it in, but first… She opened her email and scrolled through, the killer's newest taunt jumping out at her almost immediately. "No."

"What's wr—"

"No. No, no, no. This isn't right." Visions of the newest murder scene battered her. She scrolled faster. "It's not right. He can't—"

That victim should have had five more days to live. Addison should have had five more days to figure out who the killer was and stop him. But he hadn't stuck to her schedule. And now another woman was dead. Because of her. She should have known, should have realized when he'd sent her the green stone. On some level, she had, even though she couldn't accept it.

Acid churned in her empty stomach. Deep sobs racked her body. She wrapped her arms around herself, clutching her body as she rocked back and forth, trying to ease the unendurable ache.

"Come on, Addison." Jace put an arm around her, gently taking the cell phone from her hand. "Do you want a drink of water?"

Her stomach turned over, and she shook her head.

"I have to call Connor. Will you be okay for a minute?"

She nodded.

He stayed close to her as he made the call and forwarded a copy of the email to Connor. "Come on. Let's go sit down and talk."

"No."

"Addison..."

"I don't want to talk." She couldn't. The images would be forever seared into her brain. The woman's long, dark hair fanned out around her in a pool of blood. The blood-spattered garden stone, seemingly carelessly discarded against the stockade fence surrounding the small garden. Only she knew the truth, that the stone had been carefully placed, meticulously arranged to match Addison's crime scene perfectly.

The woman's wide blue eyes, filled with fear, pleading for her life, begging for him to spare her. Addison had looked into those eyes, deep into them, desperately searching for a reflection of the killer, for an image of the monster she'd unleashed.

She couldn't talk about those images. Not with anyone, but especially not with Jace. The sympathy in his eyes would be her undoing. The compassion. The lack of blame she knew she shouldered. She didn't deserve compassion. Only his victims did.

Jace didn't argue. He turned over an empty laundry basket, plopped down on an overstuffed chair in the corner and propped his feet up on the basket.

"I'm going to bed. I need to sleep." *Or just cry my eyes out without an audience.*

"I'm not leaving you alone, so forget it. Connor is calling the lawyer. He'll forward Austin the email, along with the others you've received up until now, and Austin will go to the detectives with all of it." He folded his arms and leaned back in the chair, apparently settling in for a while.

Fine. Let him. She probably wouldn't sleep anyway, but there was no denying his presence made her feel safer. Guilt struck hard. Where did she get off worrying about her own safety when three women had already died? Three of the four who'd die before the killer went after Maris.

Her breath hitched.

How long did she have? If the killer decreased the time frame between murders, he'd get to Maris a whole lot sooner than expected. "You have to tell Connor to get Maris out of here."

"He'll take care of Maris."

"No. You don't understand." Sobs tore free. She had no hope of reining them in, so she tried to talk through them. "She's the only victim we can prevent from being killed, the only one we can anticipate and protect. She has to go into hiding."

A small smile played at the corner of his mouth. "You try telling her that."

Her temper flared. "This isn't a joke, Jace."

He held up his hands. "I know it's not a joke. But Maris is as safe as we can make her. Or, at least, as safe as she'll allow us to make her. Believe me, Connor said he's tried, more than once, to get her to agree to a safe house. It's not happening. Unless you want me to knock her out and drag her there, which would be fine with me…"

He paused, looking a little too hopeful, so she settled for glaring at him.

When she didn't answer, he simply shrugged and moved on. "We'll do the best we can to protect her. In the meantime…" He leaned forward, resting his elbows on his knees and clasping his hands. "We need to figure out who he is and stop him before he kills anyone else."

"And what about your feelings for Maris? Will they interfere with you protecting her?"

His expression hardened, danger darkening his eyes. Funny, since she'd gotten to know him better, it had seemed he was a lot less menacing than she'd first thought. The edge in his eyes, along with the harsh angle of his clenched jaw made her reassess that impression. This was a dangerous man. She'd do well to remember that.

"First of all, my personal feelings would never interfere with me protecting someone. Anyone. Ever." He held her gaze, his hard stare holding her captive. Then he sighed, and his expression softened. "Besides, it seems my feelings about your sister have gotten a bit complicated. While I'm still angry with her for what she did, I'm starting to understand the why of it a little better. And maybe I don't blame her as much as I once did."

"So you like her more now?"

He stared into her eyes. "Don't push it."

She nodded. At least he'd given some. And he was going to help her, so that was all that really mattered. And with time, maybe he'd even forgive Maris, as Addison had. "But you will try to keep her safe?"

"I'll do what I can."

That would have to be good enough. She'd gotten to know Jace enough by now that she figured he'd protect all of them at any cost, but with the chaos threatening to consume her right now, she'd needed the reassurance.

"Now, if you're not going to talk to me about any of this, why don't we get some rest?" He stretched, then grunted, wincing as he gripped his side.

"Are you all right?"

"Yeah. Just a little sore."

"Here, let me check it for you." She led him to the bathroom, took bandages and tape from the medicine cabinet and set them on the counter, then peeled the tape from the wound on his side, taking care not to rip off any skin. It looked clean. No puss, no sign of infection. But still… "It doesn't seem too bad, but you should probably have it looked at."

He waved off her concern. "I'll just keep it bandaged so it stays clean, and it'll be fine."

She huffed out a breath. As much as she hated to admit it, Jace Montana was growing on her. She put antibiotic ointment on the wound, bandaged him back up and rolled his T-shirt back down.

His stare weighed heavily, and she didn't dare lift her gaze to his eyes. The urge to kiss him, to lose herself in his embrace, to escape for even a moment—

She jerked back. The last thing she needed was a complication like Jace. "There. That's the best I can do. But you should still see a doctor. You probably need a tetanus shot or something."

"I had one a few years ago when I stepped on a rusty nail."

She put the bandages away and fled the bathroom, needing space, needing to escape the heat he generated in the small room. A dull headache throbbed in her temples. She pulled the elastic band from her hair, dropped it onto the nightstand and grabbed pajama pants and a T-shirt from her drawer. She didn't have to turn around to know he'd followed her. His presence dominated the room, making the generous space feel too small. Claustrophobia threatened. "I'm going in the bathroom to get changed."

She didn't wait for a response, simply went into the bathroom and closed the door behind her. Then she caught her reflection in the mirror. Bloodshot and swollen eyes, puffy red cheeks, raw from wiping away more tears than she'd shed since she was a child and—

She jerked her gaze away from the mirror. She needed a shower and some rest. And she had to push aside her feelings and bury them deep in a small corner of her heart no one would ever touch. That shouldn't be too hard. She'd certainly had enough practice.

And then she needed to figure out who the killer was. Jace was right. She should be able to get inside his head. After all, her book had inspired him.

When Addison returned to the bedroom, Jace kept his distance, not wanting her to feel cornered. "Are you all right?"

"I'm fine, thank you."

He started toward her. "Addison—"

"Jace, stop. Please. I don't want your pity." She pressed the heels of her hands against her eyes. "I can't handle it."

"That's one thing you won't get from me."

She let her hands flop to her sides. "What's that?"

"Pity," he whispered. He inched toward her, slowly, careful not to startle her, and stopped just short of reaching out for her, leaving only a couple of inches between them.

She stiffened.

He froze where he was but made no attempt to pull back. He kept his hands at his sides, though the urge to pull her into his embrace was almost impossible to resist. "I don't pity you. I feel bad you're having a rough time right now. I wish you trusted me enough to tell me what's going on in your head. And I will do what I can to help you, but not out of pity."

"Don't you have something better to do?"

He ignored the flash of anger in her eyes in favor of the pain that raged beneath it.

His preconceived image of her, based on her affiliation not only with Maris but with Brandon, as well, had been way off. He'd never expected her strength, her compassion or her courage. The fire in her eyes touched him in a way nothing else had in a long time. He'd sorely underestimated Addison Keller.

"Women are dying because of me," she whispered.

"They are not dying because of you. They're dying because someone is killing them." And he had every intention of finding out who that someone was and stopping him. "There's a difference."

"Oh, really? Because I'm having a hard time seeing it." She lowered her gaze and shook her head.

"You suspect him, don't you." It wasn't a question. Not really. He could see the truth in her eyes a fraction of a second before she averted her gaze. "Brandon. You think he has something to do with this."

She shrugged.

"Why? Because you actually think he's involved, or because you want to see him put away? Because you have some reason to believe he killed these women or because you're afraid of him and want him behind bars where he can't hurt you?" He approached slowly. When she didn't retreat, he smoothed back a few strands of hair that had fallen into her face.

The bruise Brandon had left on her face stood out starkly against her pale skin. He couldn't deny wanting justice for himself, but he was beginning to want it for Addison more. He cleared his throat, anger that Brandon had ever gotten close to her nearly choking him.

She lowered her gaze. "It would be just like him. To find what I love and take it from me, sully it, ruin it. Turn it into something sick and evil and twisted. Like him." She finished on the softest whisper of sound. "But he…"

"But he what?"

"Nothing."

Her pulse fluttered beneath his lingering touch. "Talk to me, Addison. Let me help. Please."

She shook her head but held his gaze. Her green eyes darkened.

He cradled the back of her head and moved closer. The longing that had first flared in the car rushed back full force. The need to have her in his arms, to keep her close to him, to reassure himself she was safe. To protect her.

He backed up. What was he thinking? "I'm sorry, I…"

She shook her head. "It's okay. I just, I…can't… I—"

"It's all right. You don't have to explain." He struggled for control. What was wrong with him? Her vulnerability tugged at him relentlessly. But how could he ask for her trust when he'd failed the last woman who'd trusted him so miserably? He didn't deserve someone like Addison, or anyone, really.

"I just think—"

He held up his hands and backed into the doorway. "I won't deny I'm attracted to you, Addison." Total understatement. "You're a beautiful woman. Inside and out."

Her cheeks flared bright red.

"But I promise to keep my hands…and my lips…to myself." He grinned. "Deal?"

She nodded, her smile tentative.

"You're even more beautiful when you smile, you know."

Shaking her head, she laughed. "You're not off to a good start."

"You're right. I'll do better. Promise." He winked and turned to go. A good run with Phoenix, right after he checked in with Connor, would put things back in perspective.

"Jace?"

He stopped and turned back to her. "Yeah?"

She stood with her arms folded, hugging herself tightly. "What would happen if you did take Brandon down?"

"What do you mean?"

"What would you do?" She rubbed her hands up and down her arms as if freezing, but her gaze remained fully focused on him. "Would you go back to the police force?"

He got the distinct impression his answer mattered to her. A lot. "Being a cop is all I've ever truly wanted to do, Addison. It's who I am. I can't change that."

She nodded and turned away.

Jace resisted the urge to go to her, to comfort her and tell her everything would be okay. He had no idea how things would turn out. And he'd never lie to her. So he walked away, her intense distrust of anyone in an SCPD uniform his dreaded companion.

THIRTEEN

Desperate for air, Addison yanked the pillow off her head then turned over and bolted upright. Her legs tangled in the blanket and sheet, and she tugged wildly, frantic to free herself.

The bedroom door flung open and Phoenix scrambled toward the bed.

"Hold on." Jace put his hands over hers. "Let me help."

She stilled, yanking her hand back, but allowing him a moment to free her from the tangle of covers. As soon as he did, she staggered to her feet.

Jace opened the window, letting the cool breeze wash over her.

She stumbled across the room and rested her hands on the sill, then lowered her head between her arms. She'd have to remember to put the screen back in, but, for now, she needed the freedom the open window brought. At least it chased away the worst of the claustrophobia. Her heart hammered painfully, and she rubbed her chest in an effort to ease the ache, knowing it wouldn't help. It never did.

She let her eyes fall shut, inhaling deeply, filling her lungs with the scents of salt and pine. The scents of home. Of comfort. The images that plagued her nightmares played out on the backs of her lids, and her eyes shot open.

Strong hands landed on her shoulders.

She jerked away and spun toward him.

Jace lifted his hands and kept them where she could see them. "It's all right, Addison. I won't hurt you. You're safe, now, but I need you to move away from the window, okay?"

"Don't you get it?" She'd worked so hard to put her life back together. And she wanted more, wanted to step out of the shadows and become part of the community, make friends, get married, raise a family, adopt a puppy. Could she do all of that with Jace? *Detective* Montana of the SCPD? Her heart stuttered. "I'll never be safe. He'll never let me have a life."

"Talk to me. Let me help you."

She shook her head. What could he do? No one could take on Brandon and win. She should have realized that. Not that she hadn't known it all along in her head, but she'd allowed herself the delusion of being able to beat him. And now she had a killer on her heels, as well.

"Do you honestly think Brandon is to blame for the murders?"

She had no clue. She turned back to the view out the window. Night had fallen while she'd slept, and moonlight spilled across the yard. Branches swayed in the soft sea breeze. The scene should offer the illusion of safety, of peace. It didn't.

Phoenix nudged her hand with his head and sat beside her.

She twined her fingers into his soft fur, taking the comfort he offered.

"Why don't you go back to bed? You didn't sleep very long."

She took a step toward him, intent on slipping into his arms, then stemmed the instinctive reaction. The fact that she wanted his comfort, wanted desperately to sink into his embrace and allow him to chase away her fears was dangerous. That fear might be the only thing that would keep her alive, might be the one thing that would motivate her enough to do anything she had to in order to protect Maris. "Why bother? It's not like I could sleep anyway."

"Okay, then, there's something else we need to talk about, something I think might help you stop the nightmares." He gestured toward the chair. "Why don't you sit down?"

She started to protest, but the grim expression on his face stopped her. "What happened?"

She perched on the edge of the seat, ready to bolt if she didn't like where this conversation headed.

"Nothing happened, exactly. But one of Connor's men uncovered an old murder that seemed…similar to the first murder in your book and the first real murder." He narrowed his eyes, obviously expecting some sort of reaction from her.

"So?"

He huffed out a breath and propped his hands on his hips, then studied her intently. With a sigh, he squatted in front of her and took her hands in his. "It was your mother's murder, Addison."

A strangled cry escaped before she could stop it.

Jace squeezed her hands, lending her his strength. "Do you remember anything about that day?"

She shook her head, because she couldn't remember. If she allowed herself, she might remember everything with vivid clarity, but it was a reminiscence she couldn't dare indulge in. If she did, she'd no longer be able to deny the truth. A giant wall slammed down on her mind, halting even the slightest thought of the past. Was that sinful? Did "Thou shalt not lie" include lying to herself? *Forgive me, Lord.*

She shot to her feet. "It was a long time ago."

Jace stepped back. "I think you could still remember if you tried."

She backed away from him. She needed the feel of his strong arms around her. She had to get away from him. "I said I don't remember."

"Talk to me, Addison. Please. I can't help you if I don't know what's going on. Please. Tell me something. Anything."

"I can't tell you what I don't remember." Images battered her defenses. She turned away from them.

"Addison—"

"I appreciate you trying to help, but I need you to leave now." *Before I lose myself in you.* For the first time in as long as she could remember, she trusted someone, trusted Jace, but she had to stay away from him. His feelings showed plainly in his expression. He was beginning to care for her. And she appreciated that he respected her enough to rein in his emotions. "I don't—"

"Please, Addison. Let me help. Talk to me."

She pressed her back against the cool wall. What did she have to offer him? Her life was a mess. He'd already been shot because of her, and chances were if he hung around, he'd end up hurt again. Or worse. Jace was a man who met danger head-on to protect those he cared about. She prayed for the strength to resist him. She had to resist him if she was going to keep him safe.

"Tell me. Please."

She lowered her gaze from his and squeezed her eyes closed. For the first time, she lowered the wall she'd built to protect herself from the truth. Memories pummeled her, unexpectedly familiar since she'd been dreaming about them for most of her life. "He came into the house."

"Who did?"

She shook her head. "I don't know."

The memory was there, the soft sound of an intruder's footsteps when no one else should have been home, but she couldn't put a face to the person. At least, not yet. That image was either buried deeper than the rest or didn't exist. "We were in the kitchen. We were going to spend the weekend together, just the two of us. We were going to bake and had just started getting everything out when we heard the footsteps crossing the living room floor."

Jace seemed to hold his breath, waiting for her response, but remained silent.

She couldn't decide if that was a good thing or not. She'd have welcomed the distraction, just one more way to avoid what she'd already avoided for too long.

"My mother opened the bottom cabinet where she kept the pans, pulled them out and pushed me inside. She whispered, 'Stay quiet no matter what, and don't come out. I love you, princess,' and closed the door. Those were the last words she ever said to me."

Tears poured down her cheeks, but she made no move to wipe them away. Her mother deserved those tears.

She'd peeked then, through the tiniest sliver of space where she'd cracked the cabinet door open. She could see his feet, his legs. "He asked if anyone else was home."

Tremors shook her. Her legs went rubbery, almost giving out.

Jace wrapped his arms around her, holding her up, willing her to be strong.

"She said no. She lied to him. The last words she ever said were a lie. A lie to protect me." The thought tortured her, had even then. Because even at three, she'd known lying was wrong. Her mom had instilled that in her. "She was a good woman, a good mother. But her last words were a lie. Do you think God forgave her that? Think He'd have offered the reward of Heaven when her last words were a lie? A sin?"

Sobs racked her body. Pain pierced her heart.

Jace smoothed her hair, soothing, comforting. "Yes, I do. It seems to me, the woman you've described would have prayed for forgiveness even as she uttered the lie, even as she prayed for God to protect her child, to save you. He answered one. Why not the other?"

She searched his expression. "Do you really believe that?"

"Of course I do."

Hope surged through her. She stared deep into his eyes and found only honesty. "Thank you for that, Jace."

She should have realized that on her own. God always forgave. It was people who had a hard time pardoning, as she'd done with Maris. She'd thought she'd stopped resenting her sister, but had she, truly, deep in her heart? And at the end of the day, what was there to forgive? Maybe her problem wasn't in forgiving Maris but in forgiving herself. It was easier to hold Maris responsible for doing what Addison should have had the courage to do, to hold on to her anger toward a woman who'd only tried to help her, rather than to face the truth, accept responsibility and seek to absolve herself.

He wrapped his arms around her waist, pulled her close and kissed the top of her head. "I'll take care of you, Addison. I'll keep you safe. And we will get to the bottom of this."

She nodded against him, her tears spilling freely, grateful he hadn't pushed her beyond what she was ready to face.

"We'll figure it all out." He held her like that while she cried, waiting with all the patience in the world while years of pent-up emotions poured out of her.

"I'm sorry," she whispered against him. Sorry she'd given him such a hard time in the beginning, sorry she hadn't trusted him, sorry he'd been hurt because of her, sorry she'd held him at arm's length when he'd tried to comfort her.

He smoothed a hand over her hair. "You have nothing to be sorry for."

Jace waited while she collected herself, enjoying the feel of her safely cocooned in his embrace where nothing could touch her. Reality would intrude soon enough and he'd have to let her go, but for just a moment, he could give her this, could take it for himself.

Addison looked at him. "So, what happens now?"

Though her eyes were red and puffy, tears still darkening her thick lashes, she seemed okay, surprisingly okay, considering the circumstances. Her courage never ceased to amaze him. "You have to talk to me. At least, try to answer my questions so we can stop the killer and Brandon, whether or not they turn out to be one and the same."

She nodded and sucked in a shaky breath, then stepped back. "What do you want to know?"

Ever since he'd seen the scar on her back, and Maris

had alluded to Brandon abusing her, Jace had wanted to ask. "What happened to your back?"

"I'll tell you, but can we sit down first?"

"Of course." He accepted the request for what it most likely was, a ploy to allow her a moment to gather her thoughts or her courage, maybe both. He had no doubt she'd find the strength she needed to do what came next. It seemed she always did. He waited for her to sit on the edge of the bed, then pulled the chair close enough to sit face-to-face with her. "Do you want something to drink first—water, maybe?"

She shook her head and lowered her gaze.

"Tell me."

"It was Brandon."

Anger like he'd never known coursed through him.

"We'd had a flood in the kitchen, and someone from the insurance company called the house. They needed information to process the claim, easy enough for me to answer their questions rather than bothering Brandon at work. I wrote down the information they needed and told the woman I'd call her back." Her breath hitched. "I'd just started to shuffle through some papers on his desk when he walked in. I didn't even know he was there. He snuck up behind me, grabbed me, told me if he ever found me in his office or going through his papers again, he'd kill me. Then he drew a knife along my back, fairly deep."

Her hands trembled wildly, but she didn't shed a single tear. "I promised him I'd never do it again and apologized up and down. I think the only thing that saved me in the end was the fact I'd written down what the woman had asked for, proof I wasn't lying to him."

That man would never lay a hand on her again, and that was a vow Jace had every intention of keeping.

"He left me there like that while he went into the other room to call someone. When he was done, he came back, dragged me to the car and took me to a house with a small clinic attached. It was in a very bad neighborhood, and I'm not even sure the man we saw was really a doctor. Brandon ordered him around and insisted he stitch me up with only a minimal scar, bad enough to ensure I remembered my promise, but not bad enough to be unattractive to him. Why should he suffer for my wrongs?"

Sensing she was done talking, whether or not the story ended there, Jace rubbed a thumb back and forth over her fingers, then brought her hand to his lips and placed a soft kiss on her knuckles. "I'm sorry."

She frowned. "What for?"

A million things, but the one he most regretted was burying his head in the sand while Brandon abused his power and used it to hurt whomever he pleased. To hurt Addison. To possibly hurt Jennifer. "For not stopping him sooner."

"I'm sorry I accused you of being involved in his crimes. I shouldn't have done that. I didn't even know you."

"You were right not to trust me…"

She stiffened.

After all, he hadn't even managed to keep his own wife safe. She'd died because of him, because he hadn't had the courage to turn to God instead of a bottle, hadn't had the strength to go home and deal with his problems instead of drowning them at a bar. "You didn't know me, and if I'm going to be honest, that was a big part of the problem. Everyone assumed I was involved in what he was doing. And I'm not going to lie. It hurt. Badly. People I'd known my entire career, longer in some cases, and they looked at me like I was a criminal. So I walked away, and in doing so, allowed him to continue unimpeded."

"That's not true. What could you have done?"

What could he have done? The question had tortured him since the day he'd resigned. He'd allowed Brandon to tarnish his good name and ruin his reputation. Brandon had cost him a career he'd loved, and Jace had done nothing.

And while he shouldered the blame for sitting in a bar while his wife was killed, though he had not one single shred of proof that Brandon had anything to do with her murder, he still couldn't help but think that if he had stopped Brandon, he might have saved her. Could he have? The answer still eluded him.

Brandon had too much power, too much influence. People feared him, and no one dared cross him. How had Jace missed that? The man was supposed to have been a friend. How could Jace have misjudged his true nature so badly?

"Brandon manipulates people, Jace. He surrounds himself with two kinds of people, those who go along with him and his schemes, and those who are truly good people. The kind of people who expect him to be what he appears to be on the surface, the kind who don't look for deception in their friends, the kind who are quick to trust. He manipulates them, lies to them and makes them believe he's genuine."

"For what purpose? Why not just align himself with criminals like himself?"

"Because he's smart. Because he can get away with doing whatever he wants while good people vouch for him. Brandon Carlisle is not a good man."

Wasn't that the understatement of the year. "I wish

I could go back and change the past, but I can't. All I can do now is ask forgiveness and pray for better judgment going forward."

She nodded.

Okay, this was going to be painful. "Thanks to Maris. She had the courage and the character to stand up and do what neither of us could."

"I owe her a tremendous apology."

"So do I, it seems." And he would offer it the minute he saw her. She'd earned his gratitude and his respect. Seemed he had his own lessons to learn about forgiveness and judging people.

Maris had been young and had implicated innocent people in her attempt to stop Brandon. While that was wrong, and hopefully she'd learned from the experience, her heart had been in the right place, and at least she'd found the courage to stand up for what she believed was right.

Phoenix, who'd been lying on the floor beside the bed, lurched to his feet and barked.

"Get down and stay there." He tucked Addison between the bed and the chair, grabbed his gun from the nightstand and pressed his back against the wall beside the window, kicking himself for having left it open.

A car door slammed. Then another.

Jace chanced a quick peek from behind the curtains. A police cruiser sat in the driveway, and two officers stood beside it, looking at the house. One of them looked over his shoulder and nodded toward a car parked across the street. A silhouette sat in the driver's seat, but Jace couldn't make out any features, couldn't even discern if it was a man or a woman. Brandon?

Phoenix barked again and jumped up, his front paws landing on the windowsill.

"Phoenix, no. Down, boy."

The big dog dropped instantly and looked at Jace.

"Addison, take Phoenix and go into the bathroom. Now. And stay low."

"Come on, boy." Addison obeyed instantly, scrambling toward the bathroom door with Phoenix beside her, keeping her head down.

"Lock the door and stay there until I come back up."

She nodded.

"Phoenix, stay."

Once they were secured inside the bathroom, Jace started across the room, then paused. Thinking better of answering the door with a loaded weapon, he dropped the pistol onto the nightstand beside the bed.

The peal of the doorbell shattered the strained silence.

Jace dialed Connor's number as he jogged down the stairs. If they were arresting Addison again, she'd need the lawyer present when she arrived at the police station. No answer. He briefly considered ignoring the door, grabbing Addison and going on the run, but he might be putting her in even more danger that way. He dialed Connor again. "Come on, Connor, pick up, man."

His stubbornness where Maris was concerned now cost him dearly. If not for his own grudge, he'd have her number in his phone. As it was, who else could he call? The lawyer. He dialed the number. When Austin's voice mail came on, Jace blurted a quick message and hung up. Now what? Nothing. He trusted no one else. He was on his own.

Wait. That's not true. For the second time since Jace fell into a bottomless well of despair, he prayed with all his heart. Prayed for forgiveness, for strength, for courage, and most of all, he prayed for Addison's safety.

He stuffed the phone into his pocket, wishing he hadn't left his gun behind, and ripped the door open.

The two officers stood on the front porch. The older one stood tall, his gaze level and confident. His younger partner kept glancing over his shoulder, sweat running in rivers down his face.

Divide and conquer? Possibly.

"What can I do for you gentlemen?"

The older officer shoved him back into the room, stepped in after him, waited for his partner to cross the threshold, then slammed the door behind him. "Don't play games with me, Montana."

Jace swallowed any argument and held his hands in front of him, palms forward. "I don't know what you're talking about. Is there something I can help you with, Officer?"

"Turn around and put your hands on the wall."

"What?" He had to be kidding.

"You're under arrest. I said turn and put your hands on the wall, and I won't say it again." He shoved Jace toward the wall at his side.

"Arrest? Me? For what?" Jace stumbled and reached out a hand to catch himself.

"Did you just take a swing?"

"What?" What on earth could they be arresting him for? Had another anonymous tip come in? Was the killer, Brandon or someone else, trying to get him out of the way so he could get to Addison?

"You saw that, right, Koenig?"

The younger officer took off his hat and wiped the sweat from his brow with his arm. "Huh?"

His partner shot him a glare. "I said, you saw him just take a swing at me when I tried to arrest him. Right?"

"Oh…" Koenig fitted his hat back on and glanced at Jace, then quickly averted his gaze.

Great, no help there.

"Koenig." That one word held not only a warning, but a not-so-veiled threat.

"Uh-huh." He nodded, keeping his gaze glued to the floor.

Decision time. If Jace let the officers take him, Addison would be left with only Phoenix for protection. If Brandon or the killer wanted her, they'd get her, and Phoenix would most likely die protecting her. If it was Jace that Brandon was after, he might leave Addison alone until Connor showed up. *Fight or comply? Stand my ground or run? God, please help me. Please stand with me and grant me the wisdom to make the right choice.*

The older officer grabbed his shoulder and pushed him toward the wall. "Last warning. Hands on the—"

Jace whirled, shoved a small console table toward the officer and turned to run.

Two-hundred-plus pounds plowed into Jace's back, taking him down hard.

His head slammed against the floor. Blackness encroached.

The officer's knee dug into his back, pinning him down.

Jace swung behind him, wrapped an arm around the man's leg and yanked it up, knocking the man off balance as he tried to roll.

Koenig fell on him, pinned him back down with a knee on his shoulder, stronger than Jace would have expected.

They cuffed his hands behind his back, then yanked him up off the floor by his cuffed hands.

His shoulders screamed in protest. Rage coursed through him. He shoved it aside. No time for that. Focus. His head swam. Blood flowed from a cut on his forehead, impeding his vision.

The officers each had an arm, caging him between them as they dragged him toward the door.

He had to escape. Had to warn Addison. Had to get Connor.

Koenig opened the front door and they hauled him through.

The car that had been parked across the street was gone. Maybe Brandon had left? Maybe it hadn't even been him. A shove from behind caught Jace off guard, and he stumbled. The officers released him, and he tumbled down the porch steps to the walkway.

The older officer leaned over him. "Mr. Carlisle would like to have a word."

Dazed and confused, Jace wasn't able to fight as they hauled him up and shoved him into the back of the patrol car. If Brandon intended to meet him somewhere, Addison was probably safe for the moment. Unless Brandon wasn't the killer.

Surely, she'd have tried to reach Maris by now. Connor would get to her. And if he couldn't, he'd send someone to protect her.

Jace's head rocked with the motion of the car. His stomach turned over. He should have dealt with Brandon in the first place, should have faced his problems head-on, with the conviction and confidence that God would help him through if he did the right thing. Regret weighed heavily.

He jerked himself upright. No way was he giving up. Maybe he'd walked away last time because the time wasn't right. Maris had tried to take him down. There hadn't been enough evidence to go after Brandon. But now... Maybe now was different. Maybe this had been God's plan all along.

Jace sat up straighter, working to clear the fog. He had to get his head clear. Addison. Her smile filled his mind. Even in his vision, despite the smile, sadness filled her eyes. He had to get to her. He had to protect her. He had to keep her safe. Because Addison Keller was an amazing woman, a strong woman who wouldn't rest until Brandon was put away this time, no matter what happened to Jace. And Maris would help her, would stand by her side as she always had, even when it meant backing off and giving her space to figure out what she needed. And Connor would, of course, look after both of them.

Despite the comfort that thought brought, he couldn't deny the absolute truth. He didn't want anyone else to stand at Addison's side. He wanted to do it himself. It had been a very long time since he'd known someone like her, someone he could admire and trust, someone he wanted to share his life with, build a future with. To love. His heart stopped. *Love.* Did he really love Addison? He did, he realized, with all of his heart. The revelation came with all of the pain and regret that they'd never get a chance to explore that love.

The car stopped, bringing another wave of nausea.

The officers dragged him from the back seat.

Then again, maybe God had given him a second chance after all.

His legs buckled. Sheer determination kept him on his feet.

"So we meet again, Jace." Brandon slunk from the shadows like the monster he was, holding a gun out in front of him aimed squarely at Jace's chest. "I tried, you know, tried to make you see reason, get you to join me. You could have had a good life, but no. No, you wanted something more, it seems. Was she worth it, Jace? Was my wife worth sacrificing yourself for?"

Yes! The knowledge came with no hesitation. Jace stood straighter, his hands cuffed behind him, blood stinging his eyes.

"Freeze!"

Connor?

Jace read his intention in the instant before Brandon fired.

He dropped and rolled.

Another gunshot, and Brandon went down. Officers swarmed around him, blocking Jace's view.

Koenig knelt over Jace. "Are you all right?"

Bright lights burned Jace's eyes.

"Jace?" Koenig grabbed his arm. "Jace? Are you all right? Are you hit?"

"What?" He tried to roll over. Needles pinched every inch of his skin. "What?"

No. Not needles. Glass. Shards of glass from broken bottles scattered across the parking lot.

"I need a medic," Koenig yelled to someone Jace couldn't see beyond the blinding light.

"Jace!"

Koenig moved away.

"Jace." Connor dropped to his knees in the carpet of glass at Jace's side. "Ah, man, Jace, are you hit? How bad?"

"Connor?" Jace struggled to sit up. Pain tore through his left shoulder. He must have dislocated it when he fell. He focused on it, using it to pull him back from the brink of darkness. "What?"

"It's all right. Everything's all right. We got him."

"Brandon?" Jace struggled to sit up.

Connor kept a hand on his arm. "Don't move. The paramedics are here now."

Jace dismissed them. "I'm okay. Just help me up."

"Were you hit?"

He took stock. His shoulder would definitely need attention at some point, but not just yet. "No. I don't think so."

"Your head."

"That was from before. I hit it." With his head beginning to clear, questions bombarded him. One more than any other. "Is Addison okay?"

"She's still home, and we have someone watching the house, but we haven't gone in. We wanted to make sure we had him first, just in case he had anyone keeping an eye on her."

"I have to get to her." He wanted to be the one to tell her it was over, wanted to see the relief in her eyes, wanted to hold her and comfort her.

"Are you sure you're all right?" Connor gripped his good arm and helped him to his feet, brushed some of the clinging glass away, and studied his eyes.

"Yeah, I'm fine." Activity swarmed around him, mostly silhouettes against the bright backdrop of spotlights. "What happened?"

Koenig appeared from behind one of the lights and uncuffed him. "Are you sure you're all right?"

Jace nodded and cradled his injured arm against him, thankful for the blessed relief that came with getting his hands out from behind him. "Thank you."

Koenig started away, then turned back. "I'm sorry I had to let him push you around like that. Believe me, if I could have stopped him, I would have."

"No problem." Jace held out a hand.

Koenig shook it, then walked away.

"He's a good man." Connor watched him go. "He was wired, so I could hear everything that went on inside that house, and let me tell you, allowing that to go on was one of the hardest things I've ever had to do."

"It doesn't matter. As long as you got him." Jace would have done whatever it took to bring down Brandon and keep Addison safe.

Connor took Jace's good arm and gestured toward a less active side of the crime scene. "I have a few good friends in Internal Affairs, men who served with me. They reached out and asked for help coordinating an operation to take Brandon down. The corruption in the department was too extensive for them to trust anyone, and they needed to get Brandon out of the way before they could weed through his associates."

"You didn't tell me." And it hurt that Connor hadn't trusted him enough to be honest.

"We thought it best not to. I'm sorry, Jace, and it had nothing to do with trust. I trust you with my life, and even more so with Addison's life, but we expected him to go after you after the incident at the police station. He was apparently pretty messed up over the fact he thought you and Addison were together. Because Internal Affairs had suspected your involvement after Brandon framed you the last time, they insisted you not be told what was going on. It was a condition they wouldn't concede."

Jace nodded. What Connor had actually given him was the chance to clear his name, to prove himself. "Do they think he's the killer?"

Connor ran a hand over his head and looked out across the crime scene. "We don't know for sure. As usual, there's no proof he's involved, but we suspect he is."

Jace only nodded. What more could he say? "I need to get to Addison."

Connor unlocked his car and guided Jace into the passenger seat, then went around and got in. When he went to start the car, he hesitated. "When this all clears, they're going to offer you your job back."

The one thing he'd wanted so badly. The one thing that would end any chance of a future with Addison. A surge of emotions threatened to drown him.

FOURTEEN

Phoenix whimpered, his soulful eyes searching Addison's for answers she didn't have.

"I know, boy." She closed her eyes and listened, reaching out with all of her senses for any hint of a sound or movement. Still nothing. "It's been too long."

Phoenix paced, his nails clicking against the tile floor.

"You stay here, boy." She couldn't wait in there any longer. With no clue when—or if—Jace was coming back, she had to at least try to get help. What if he was lying injured downstairs, unable to call out? Addison slid from the bathroom, careful not to let Phoenix out. She'd thought briefly of taking him for protection, but she'd never forgive herself if something happened to him.

With one hand on the bedroom door handle, Addison listened again. Silence roared back at her. She took a few tentative steps toward the window. Keeping to the side as she'd seen Jace do, she peeked out.

A dark sedan sat empty across the street. Streetlights stood sentinel down the otherwise deserted road.

Phoenix barked and jumped against the door.

She whirled toward him and barreled into a large man she'd never seen before.

A sick grin split his thick beard. "Hello, Addison. Remember me?"

"No," she whispered, backpedaling until her back hit the wall. Memories slammed the protective wall she'd built to shield her mind from the past. "No, it can't be."

He pulled a long cord from his pocket and wrapped one end around each of his hands. "I was willing to leave you alone, you know. If you had just kept your mouth shut."

"I don't know what you're talking about." She held her hands up in front of her, pleading, searching frantically for some way out. She had to escape. *Please, God, help me.*

"The game is over, Addison, and news flash, you lose." He pulled the cord taut and took a step toward her.

"Who are you? Why are you doing this?"

"Don't play stupid with me, little sis."

A tidal wave of memories washed over her, practically knocking her to her knees. She straightened her legs, willing them to hold her up. Falling now would probably condemn her to the same fate her mother had suffered all those years ago.

"Eddie," she blurted out the name before she could stop it.

"There you go."

"Why?"

"Oh, please. Did you really expect you could write a book detailing the murder you must have witnessed, put it out there for the world to see, and I wouldn't find out about it?"

"No, please, Eddie. It's not like that." She had to keep him talking, had to find a way out. Where was

Jace? Had Eddie done something to him? She opened her mouth to ask, then clamped it tightly shut again. If Jace was creeping toward them from somewhere, she didn't want to give him away. But she couldn't count on that, because he might be... No, she wouldn't even think that, couldn't bear the thought.

Eddie lunged.

She dropped, rolled away from him and scrambled to her feet.

He slammed into her back, knocking her against the nightstand.

She tried to turn, used the nightstand for leverage. It tipped, spilling its contents across the floor, and she fell over it, then tried to crawl away from him.

He fell onto her, one knee digging deep into her back.

She tried to scream but couldn't suck in enough air. Tried to turn but couldn't shake him off.

He hooked the cord over her head.

She tucked her chin, shoving one hand between the cord and her face, then swung her elbow back, landing a solid blow. The pressure eased off her back for just an instant. That was all she needed.

She dove forward, using her toes to propel herself the few feet to the wall, where Jace's gun had landed, and grabbed the weapon.

Eddie caught hold of her leg and yanked her back.

She twisted, aimed and pulled the trigger.

He jerked back, his eyes wide with shock. Blood flowed from his arm, but it barely slowed him down. He grabbed Addison's wrist and twisted.

The gun dropped from her hand, and Eddie lunged for it.

Phoenix scratched wildly against the bathroom door, barking, growling, desperate to get out.

She couldn't chance opening the door, couldn't risk him getting out while Eddie had the gun. Addison lurched to her feet and bolted for the bedroom door. She ran down the hallway, stumbled down the stairs, barely pausing at the bottom. Which way?

Eddie pounded down the stairs behind her.

The console table blocked the foyer. Out the back then. She changed direction, slid on the area rug and caught herself against the wall as Eddie reached the bottom of the stairs and fired off a shot.

Addison screamed and ducked into the kitchen, slamming her hip against the table. She ignored the pain, ripped the back door open and ran. Déjà vu assailed her as she crossed the patch of lawn. Her lungs begged for air. Her heart hammered painfully. Almost to the woods.

But what good would it do? Unlike last time, when the intruder had been content to spend some time in her bedroom, Eddie was right on her heels. She dove behind the first tree she came to, the same tree she'd hidden behind the first time she'd fled her house in the middle of the night. Only that time, Jace had shown up to save her.

Tears streamed down her face, blurring her vision. She had to get a grip.

Eddie stood framed in the back doorway, scanning the yard. He took a couple of steps, then bent at the waist and rested his hands on his knees.

The years since she'd last seen him hadn't been kind to him. Punishment for his sins? Maybe, but at the moment, it might be the only thing that saved her.

Addison squatted down, keeping as low as possible, and started to back away from the tree.

Eddie fired the weapon again. "You may as well

come out, Addison. There aren't many trees out here big enough to conceal you."

He fired again, and the bullet struck the tree she was hiding behind.

He stalked toward her.

She scrambled back and fell over a large dead branch.

Eddie reached the edge of the woods.

She wasn't going to make it. Running was no longer an option. She gripped the branch she'd fallen over, pulled it close and waited, crouched deep in the shadows.

Eddie crashed into the woods, headed straight for her.

She waited.

Closer.

She held her breath. Didn't dare move, not even to breathe. Her lungs strained.

"There you are."

She pounced, swinging the branch with all her might, landing a solid blow to his side.

He managed to hold on to the gun, and swung it around toward her.

She struck him again, this time catching him across the face.

"Don't move!" Jace held a weapon pointed right at Eddie. "Hands in the air. Now!"

Connor came up behind Jace, weapon drawn and aimed at Eddie.

Eddie whirled toward them, swinging the gun around.

Addison dove for the ground and squeezed her eyes shut tight, covering her head as the sound of gunfire tore through the night.

Memories assailed her, memories she'd buried for so long, memories she couldn't deal with, couldn't accept.

Memories her mind had shielded her from since child-hood. Memories her three-year-old mind didn't know how to come to terms with when she'd cowered in that dark cabinet and witnessed the fifteen-year-old brother she'd loved kill their mother.

"Addison!" Jace crouched beside her and lifted her hair away from her face. "Addison, look at me. Are you hurt?"

She couldn't open her eyes, couldn't bear to look. She lacked the courage to ask what she desperately needed to know. A sob tore free before she could stop it. And another.

"Addison, honey, please, talk to me. Answer me." Jace sat at her side and pulled her into his arms. "Are you hurt?"

Connor barked orders into his phone, demanding an ambulance and backup.

She didn't want an ambulance, didn't need to go to the hospital. "Phoenix?"

Jace's breath shot out, and he pulled her closer, rest-ing his chin on her head. "I think he's okay. I heard him barking like mad when we came in the front door, but I have to get to him. Are you okay?"

She took stock. Sore, and she'd probably hurt even worse tomorrow, but she would be okay. And he was right, they did have to get to Phoenix. She had to make sure he was okay, had to see for herself. She stared at Eddie's prone form. "Is he…?"

Jace looked at Connor, who shook his head. "No, just injured. Can you tell me what happened? Do you know who he is?"

She nodded against Jace's chest, not quite able to leave the comfort of his strong embrace, and cried softly. "My brother."

* * *

Jace held her until her sobs lessened, then set her back enough to look into her eyes. "Are you all right?"

She glanced at her brother, who was lying where he'd fallen, as cops hovered around and the EMTs worked on him.

Connor leaned over them. "Are you hurt?"

She shook her head. "I'm okay."

Jace helped her to her feet.

Phoenix barked and barreled through the back door and across the lawn toward them.

Maris leaned against the doorjamb, hands in her jacket pockets, smiling.

Seemed he had one more thing to add to the list he'd have to thank Maris for.

He crouched down and held his good arm open for Phoenix. The big dog launched himself at Jace, almost knocking him over. Pain tore through Jace's left shoulder, but he ignored it, needing the comfort as much as Phoenix did.

Phoenix licked his face, and Jace laughed, genuine joy rushing through him.

He kept his hand on Phoenix's head when he stood and faced Addison. So much to be grateful for, so much he didn't deserve.

A detective approached and gestured for Connor to step aside with him.

"What do you think that's about?" Addison's gaze held steady on the two.

"I don't know." And it didn't matter, he realized. Everything that mattered to him was right there. Addison, whom he tucked beneath his arm and held close, Phoenix, who'd always stood at his side, Connor, who was still his brother despite the way Jace had pulled away, and even Maris, whom he owed not only his thanks but a huge apology.

Jace took the moment to give Addison a condensed account of how he'd been kidnapped by Brandon, assuring her he was fine and that Brandon would be going away for a long time. Finally. "Connor is pretty sure they're going to offer me my job back."

She squeezed her eyes shut. When she opened them, tears shimmered in their depths. "With the SCPD?"

He nodded, searching her gaze for a clue to how she felt about that, about him, about their chances for a future together.

She lowered her gaze. "Congratulations, Jace. I couldn't be happier for you. I know how badly you want to resume your career."

He could feel her pulling away. "I'm going to say no."

"When will you know... Wait...what?"

"It seems Connor is just as persuasive as I remember." He grinned, filled with joy that he and Connor were back on track. He'd missed their friendship. "He's offered me a position with his PI firm."

"Are you serious? Are you going to say yes?"

"I am."

Addison threw her arms around his neck and hugged him.

He savored the warmth of her embrace. The feeling that all was right with his world poured through him for the first time in years.

The detective clapped Connor on the back, spared Jace a quick glance and a wave, then walked away.

Lifting his arm from around Addison, Jace waved back.

Connor returned to them, rubbed a hand over his head, then met Addison's gaze. "Eddie's talking, even though we advised him of his right to remain silent. Seems he's been keeping tabs on you all along, Addison. When your book came out, he couldn't let things go any longer and decided to use it as a model and come after you to silence you."

"So Brandon didn't have any involvement in the killings, after all?"

Connor shrugged. "He took advantage of the situation, used it to try to hurt you. It doesn't matter, though. Unfortunately, he's not confessing as freely as Eddie. We might not be able to get him for any of the murders, not even Jennifer's, but Brandon Carlisle is still going away."

"He's too smart for that," Addison mumbled.

Connor shook his head. "We've got him on kidnapping, attempted murder and assaulting both you and Jace at the police station. He's going away for a long time."

Jace pulled Addison even closer and kissed her temple. "Either way, you no longer have to live in fear of him or the killer."

She lowered her gaze. "I'm so sorry. If only I had remembered sooner, allowed myself to remember sooner…"

"Hey." Connor ran a hand up and down her arm. "None of this is your fault. Understand? Now, why don't you two go up to the house while I finish up here?"

Jace released Addison long enough to give him a one-armed hug. When he'd come through the house and heard Phoenix barking and found the back door standing open, his heart had almost stopped. Running across the lawn and finding Addison trying to fight off an armed killer played through his mind in a constant loop. "Thanks, Connor."

He nodded and walked away.

Jace started toward the house, sheltering her beneath his arm, lending her whatever strength she might need to begin to recover. "It's okay, now, Addison. It's over. The killer and Brandon."

"I wish I could..." Addison looked over at his arm, cradled against himself to keep from jarring it and sending a stab of pain spiraling through his body. She jerked back, her eyes going wide. "You're hurt. What happened?"

"I'm fine. Honest. But it's a long story, and I'll tell you everything later." He clasped her hand desperately, needing to be close to her, to feel her touch, to know she was alive and unhurt. He stood face-to-face with her on the back lawn, while crime scene techs and detectives swarmed around them.

He ignored them as he studied the concern in her eyes, concern for him, even after what she'd just been through. "You left Phoenix in the bathroom? Why?"

"I didn't want him to get hurt."

And there it was. Everything he loved about her. He'd left the big dog to protect her, and she'd been willing to fight off a killer herself rather than put him in danger. He tucked a few strands of loose hair behind her ear, then cradled her cheek in his hand. "When I was in the back of that police car, and it pulled away from the house, and I had to leave you alone here, unprotected, I thought..."

How could he explain it to her? How could he convey the extent of the emotions that had washed over him, threatened to drown him? "I love you, Addison. I know I don't deserve it, don't deserve you, but in those moments, I knew with every last bit of my heart that I love you. I understand we have obstacles to work through, but I believe we can overcome them. Together. Please say you're willing to give us a chance."

Addison closed the gap between them, slid her arms around his waist and laid her head against his heart. "I love you, Jace. I fought it as long as I could, tried so hard not to let my mind accept what my heart already knew."

He hugged her close, weaved his fingers through the soft strands of hair and kissed the top of her head. Whether he deserved it or not, and he'd have to work hard to forgive himself for the past, he'd accept this gift, accept that God had forgiven him, blessed him with a second chance.

EPILOGUE

Addison clipped Max's leash to his collar, then petted her new pup's head.

The beagle-mix puppy she'd rescued a week earlier nuzzled her hand.

"Come on, boy. Jace and Phoenix will be here to pick us up any minute." She scooped him up and hugged him close.

"You're going to spoil him." The screen door banged shut behind Maris as she strolled into the foyer. "How's he going to learn to walk on the leash if you carry him everywhere you go?"

She only cuddled Max closer and kissed his head. "He'll learn."

Maris laughed, the sound filling Addison with almost as much joy as her new puppy. "Come on, let me take him out while you finish getting ready."

Reluctant to let the puppy go, she hugged him once more. In the short amount of time he'd been with her, she'd come to love him more than she ever could have imagined. She kissed him again and handed him over to Maris. "Thank you."

"No problem." Maris gestured toward the front yard. "Hurry up and get your jacket. Jace just pulled up."

Addison had wanted to sleep in her own house, but she was reluctant to be alone, so Maris had come to stay with her for the past few weeks since their brother had been arrested, and they'd spent a considerable amount of time sitting together, talking, catching up, getting to know each other again. Repairing their relationship meant the world to Addison.

She shrugged into a light windbreaker and checked she had everything Max would need for a day of hiking.

"Knock, knock." Jace rapped his knuckles against the doorjamb and peeked through the screen. "Can I come in for a minute?"

"Of course." She hefted the bag over her shoulder. "I was just finishing up."

He walked into the foyer, slid the bag from her shoulder and lowered it to the floor beside the door. Then he took her hand, kissed her knuckles and led her through the house and out the back door.

She laughed as she fell into step at his side. "Where are we going?"

"You'll see." He wrapped an arm around her shoulder and kissed her temple. "It's beautiful out today, a nice day for a hike."

A cool breeze rustled the leaves, the crisp clean air a promise that fall was in full swing and winter wouldn't be far behind. "Are we going to hike a trail today, or do you want to walk along the beach?"

"Maris and Connor are going to meet us at the trail with Phoenix and Max in about an hour."

"Why aren't we all going together?"

Jace led her into the woods, past the tree where she'd first run into him what seemed like forever ago, past the spot where Eddie had attacked her, deeper into the woods to a small clearing. Sunlight flickered between red, orange and gold leaves, setting their brilliant colors ablaze. "I wanted a few minutes to talk to you about something."

Addison's heart stuttered. Jace had been hovering since he'd saved her, always nearby, patient when she needed space, a confidant when she needed to talk.

He gestured toward a fallen tree, and she sat, inhaling deeply the salty scent of the sea coming to her on the soft breeze.

He knelt beside her, keeping her hand in his, and brushed a gentle kiss against her knuckles. "I love you, Addison, with all of my heart. You brought me back from a place I never want to be again. A place I don't think I could have returned from on my own. With you, I've found not only love, but faith and trust, as well."

Warmth poured through her.

He hugged her tightly, then set her back a little. He pulled something from his pocket and gently took her hand in his. "I want to build a life with you, Addison, repair the cabin in Shady Creek, raise a family there together. I love you, and I want to share my life with you forever. Will you marry me?"

"Oh, Jace." He was everything she could want—strong, brave, kind, patient, the kind of man who'd make an amazing husband and father. "I would love to be your wife."

He slid a ring onto her finger, the small heart-shaped diamond reflecting the sunlight, a promise of the future he described. She couldn't wait to begin building their life together.

* * * * *

*If you enjoyed this book, pick up these other exciting
stories from Love Inspired Suspense.*

Desert Rescue
by Lisa Phillips

On the Run
by Valerie Hansen

Seeking Amish Shelter
by Alison Stone

Alaska Secrets
by Sarah Varland

Texas Witness Threat
by Cate Nolan

Find more great reads at www.LoveInspired.com

Dear Reader,

Thank you so much for sharing Jace and Addison's story! I love flawed characters, whose internal conflicts are as unique and challenging as the danger they find themselves in.

One of the things both Jace and Addison struggle with is the ability to forgive, though they seem to find it easier to forgive others than to forgive themselves. Maybe because it's easier to accept flaws in others than it is to look inside ourselves and acknowledge we've made mistakes. I think that's true for a lot of us, and it's my prayer that we can all find it in our hearts to always forgive one another and ourselves, as God teaches us, and in doing so create a stronger, kinder world.

I hope you've enjoyed sharing Jace and Addison's journey as much as I enjoyed creating it. If you'd like to keep up with me, you can find me on Facebook, www.facebook.com/DeenaAlexanderAuthor, and Twitter, twitter.com/DeenaAlexanderA.

Deena Alexander

WE HOPE YOU ENJOYED
THIS BOOK FROM

LOVE INSPIRED SUSPENSE
INSPIRATIONAL ROMANCE

Courage. Danger. Faith.

Find strength and determination in stories
of faith and love in the face of danger.

6 NEW BOOKS AVAILABLE EVERY MONTH!

Get 4 FREE REWARDS!

We'll send you 2 FREE Books plus 2 FREE Mystery Gifts.

Love Inspired Suspense books showcase how courage and optimism unite in stories of faith and love in the face of danger.

FREE
Value Over
$20
